Get Rufus!

a novel by the dean of mountain writers

Bob Terrell

In the remote Great Smoky Mountains of Western North Carolina, the sheriff of Jackson County, way back around 1917, had just two words when someone was needed to restore law and order —"get Rufus!"— and Rufus would come a ridin' into Sylva, the county seat, on his female mule, Fred, and then the fur would fly and the bad guys get their comeuppance.

Land of the Sky Books

Alexander, North Carolina

Dedication

To everyone of my old friends mentioned in this book and more.

Disclaimer

In this book, I've used some names of real persons to honor them but the characters so named do not reflect any real person's character living or dead.
—Bob Terrell

Publisher: Ralph Roberts

Cover Design: Ralph Roberts

Cover and Interior Art ©2008: Lissa Silver

Editor: Pat Roberts

Interior Design and Electronic Page Assembly: WorldComm®

Printed in the United States of America

10 9 8 7 6 5 4 3 2 1

ISBN 978-1-56664-273-6 (paperback)

ISBN 978-1-56664-274-3 (hardback)

Land of the Sky Books—a publishing imprint of Creativity, Inc.–is a full-service publisher located at 65 Macedonia Road, Alexander NC 28701. Phone (828) 252-9515 or (828) 255-8719 fax. For orders only: 1-800-472-0438. Visa and MasterCard accepted.

Land of the Sky Books is distributed to the trade by **aBOOKS** 65 Macedonia Road, Alexander NC 28701. To order, call 1-800-472-0438.

This book is also available on the Internet along with our other books. Set your browser to **http://abooks.com** and enjoy the many fine values available there.

CONTENTS

Lissa Silver©

ONE

Breakfast at the old farm house a mile up Fisher Creek where Rufus Raby lived with his mother, Paralee, was usually corn bread from the night before, warmed in the oven and buttered with butter from Paralee's churn, three or four eggs fried in deep fat, and thick slabs of bacon, with scalding black coffee to wash it down. This morning, Rufus entered the kitchen with bleary eyes and throbbing head. He muttered that he felt as bad as a burnt out stump and had a drum beating in his head. His ma said, "Set ye'self down, son."

His ma was a hard working, rather stout woman—not fat, just stout—fiftyish, with iron gray hair, the result of a lifetime of hard work on the farm. Not one to chide her son for partaking of the grape, or, in this case, the corn, she poured a mug of strong, black coffee and put it beside his plate. He worked so hard around the farm that he had to have some distraction from the work, and if he partook of his own corn whiskey, she found nothing to scold him about that. After all, the production of Rufus's still provided a large portion of their income since Rufus refused to log the poplar forests on the farm.

He dropped his tall, husky frame into his chair at the table. He was quite good looking, the womenfolk thought, with his dark eyes and complexion, a mop of dark, wavy hair, and an infectious smile that sometimes stopped unmarried girls in their tracks. His muscular build attested to his strength, acquired by years of toiling in tobacco and timber.

He was not a small man, standing above six feet and weighing in the vicinity of two hundred pounds. A heavy black beard underlay the skin of his cheeks and chin. He never arose in the morning without shaving immediately, yet the shadow of thick dark beard was never absent from his handsome features.

His mother surprised him, bringing from the oven a pan of golden-topped biscuits, light as a feather. She placed them on the table before him beside a jar of honey from their own hives, the eggs, and a slabs of bacon.

She cooked on a wood range in the kitchen, and Rufus had to provide the stove wood to feed the range every day.

"Rufus, when you get to feelin' better, you better chop some stove wood," she said, "We're runnin' low, but wait till your head clears up before you chop it. I don't want no chopped off fingers in the wood box."

Rufus squinted at his mother through bloodshot eyes, trying to clear his head of a self-inflicted drum roll from last night's bout with the fruit of his whiskey still, hidden not far away up Possum Branch. He blew cigarette smoke in a cloud over the table, and asked, "What's so special 'bout today?"

"Little surprise fer ye, son. You been working awful hard here lately."

"I know," he said, "but these here rations is for comp'ny. Ought to save 'em for a special day."

He held his forehead with a hand, swallowed long gulps of strong, black coffee, and with wrinkled brow stared at his mother, trying to focus on what she was saying. "What's so good 'bout today?"

"It's special," she said, looking wistfully out the window. "It's the day your pa and me got hitched over to Preacher Mull's house."

"When was that?" he asked.

"Let's see," she pondered. "You're nearly twenty-six now, so I guess 'bout twenty-some year ago. I reckon twenty-seven. You was borned a year after we got married up." She figured on her fingers. "This here's nineteen-seventeen," and a moment later she added, "Reckon that'd make it about ninety or ninety-one, or there'bouts, when we got hitched."

To his mother's satisfaction, he wolfed down his breakfast, savoring the biscuits smeared with butter and honey, drank half a pot of black coffee, then put on his hat and stumbled toward the door, still bleary-eyed.

"Where you bound, son?" asked his mother.

"Thought I'd go to town. Ain't been in a coon's age, seems like."

"Watch ye'self, son. I've had a bad feelin' this morning, like something's a'goin' to happen."

"What, Ma?" he asked. "What's gonna happen?"

"I don't rightly know. Ain't got that far with it yet. I'm a'hoping nothin' bad's gonna happen to you. I couldn't do much with this here farm without you, so be careful. Hear?"

"I hear, Ma," he said. "I'll be careful. I ain't gonna start trouble with nobody. Gonna ride to town and hang out a little. Maybe throw a knife or two. It's Saturday and ever'body'll be in town."

He felt for the dull, rusty knife in his pocket, and figured he would get somebody's goat, swapping it sight unseen from a clenched fist for a better blade.

He saw his ma grinning as if she knew a secret.

"What?" he asked. "Somethin' else?"

"Yes, they's somethin' else," she answered. "Happy birthday, son, if you don't get back tonight. Tomorrow's your birthday."

"Son of a gun!" he said. "Reckon it is. You got a good memory, Ma."

"No," she said, "I ain't no more, but that's something no mother forgets. Your brother would'a been twenty-two last Wednesday if he'd a'lived."

"I know," Rufus said. "He'd be alive if he hadn't braced them Hannessey boys. Weren't no call to kill him. Reckon I'll square that up some day. The law considered it a fair fight, but I don't see nothin' fair in three on one."

"You leave them boys alone." Protectively, she turned back to look at him with apprehension in her eyes. Rufus was her only son now that William was gone. "They'd get you like they got William. They's too many of 'em. Four or five, ain't they? And they ain't boys no more; they're men growed, or just the same as."

"I ain't gonna look for no trouble," he said, and under his breath he added, "but if it comes a'looking fer me, I ain't a'gonna dodge it. Besides," he said aloud, "they's only three of 'em." He took a .32 caliber revolver off a shelf, checked the loads, and tucked it in the right front pocket of his overalls.

Rufus started for the door, stopped, and turned back.

"You go ahead," his mother said. "I'll slop the hog an' milk Bessie. Go on."

Outside, with the sun about to peek over the hills that rose eastward from the far side of Fisher Creek in the rear of the house, Rufus looked about and turned his thoughts to their farm, a hundred-sixty-acre quarter-section his pa had bought from Old Man Mallonee for eight hundred dollars.

Maybe it wasn't much to the eye, not with its old, unpainted, T-shaped, frame farm house and long-weathered barn, but it was home. It was a farmhouse typical of the day. A porch stretched across the front of the house. An entrance led to a bedroom on the right and a living room on the left, followed by a dining room and a kitchen and a sizable porch on the rear of the house. The second story, above the living room and bedroom, contained two bedrooms.

The living room was equipped with a fireplace that kept the living room and all bedrooms warm in winter because of the way heat goes up. In some cases, where farmers were growing old, they placed a bed in the living room where the old man and his wife slept. In summer all windows were raised to keep the house cool with the wonderful breezes flowing down from the Balsam Mountains.

It was also something, Rufus thought, that might be turned into a better-looking place with a little money and a lot of elbow grease. Money had come from his pa's profits from his corn whiskey distillery up Possum Branch and he still had money in his pocket after buying the farm. Business had been good them days, Rufus chuckled, and said to himself, "Business ain't so bad these days, neither, but I reckon that time were special."

Rufus's pa had died soon after buying the place, some said from an overdose of his own squeezings but Rufus and his mother allowed it was the flu that got him.

The acreage was enough for Rufus and his ma, especially since he had the whiskey still, which was all but legal, he figured. Sheriff Bright, who had preceded Sheriff Clure, had looked the other way when he came near Rufus's pa's still because his pa kept the sheriff supplied free of charge with the best corn whiskey in Jackson County, and that was saying something. The mountains were filled with competition. Distilling was the most lucrative occupation in the hills these days.

Rufus always suspected that Sheriff Bright sold some of the spirits discretely to supplement his meager salary. A man had to live, Rufus thought, and he figured he knew from experience what he was talking about. After his daddy died, Rufus got to keep the still because he was the best tracker in the county who Sheriff Clure always used when trailing a fugitive on the run. By mutual agreement, Clure ignored Rufus's still and tracking cost the county nothing. Both parties figured things balanced out about even.

Rufus had replaced his pa as the best moonshine maker in Jackson County and he never exceeded the limit of gallons that Sheriff Clure had discretely included in the deal, except sometimes by a dozen gallons or so, which he secreted in the barn loft in pint and quart canning jars and gallon jugs, hidden in a small, unnoticed alcove in the loft, surrounded by heavy sacks of feed. He sold the liquor to a circle of friends, some of whom came from as far away as the head of Caney Fork to purchase Rufus's jugs. If he had any left over after his friends made their purchases, he sold it to anybody.

The deal pleased Rufus greatly since he could make enough extra whiskey to turn a profit large enough to hire help for plowing, planting, and harvesting on the farm. Work hands were easy to come by and Rufus kept the good ones, paying them two dollars a day, which was excellent money for a day's work. The farm ran from Fisher Creek to the top of the mountain in front of the house. The house faced the road and the rising sun, and on its north side were two acres of fertile bottom land on Rufus's side of Possum Branch. The small stream ran pure and clear off the Balsam Mountains to mix itself with Fisher Creek's larger flow.

A spring of good water came out of the ground between the house and Possum Branch, which provided Paralee and Rufus with pure, clear water. From the spring, the water they didn't use flowed back into Possum Branch along a channel Rufus had dug. The spring water was so good it relieved Rufus of the task of digging a well, which many families had to do if they had no access to spring water. Rufus kept the spring free of debris by cleaning it out weekly and had plans to build a spring house over it one day.

On the mountain behind the house were two large stands of virgin poplar in the midst of the pastureland and blackberry vines. Rufus preferred poplar for his fireplace; he liked the pop and crackle of the fire and the fizzing of the green wood he fed it.

The remainder of the farm included ninety acres of virgin, primeval timber which Rufus refused to log because part of it hid his still. The entire farm had been deeded to Rufus by his mother the week after his brother was slain.

Rufus liked working with saw and ax, cutting the winter's supply of firewood, so he relegated himself to the task of woodcutter, putting a young hired hand, Hovie, on the other end of the crosscut saw. Thereby Rufus put on the appearance of a working man. He also did the woodcutting because he wanted to keep workmen from thinning the poplar groves. For firewood he cut only stunted trees, the runts of the forest that did not grow as well as the tall poplar.

Rufus crossed the road and dunked his head in Fisher Creek, shook the water out of his hair, and walked past the smokehouse and the outhouse to the three-stall barn, climbing the ladder to the loft, in which he had built a drying room for his tobacco crops. Some of his crop was for his own smoking and occasional chewing and the rest to sell for cash money. As he went by, he checked the hanging tobacco in the slatted, airy room, and grinned his pleasure. Rufus screwed the lid off a quart jar of whiskey, took a long draught from the jar and smiled. "Ahhhh," he breathed. "Hair of the dog...."

Tobacco was the only income he had officially, or at least the only income he talked about. Production from his thirty-gallon copper still brought in more cash than the tobacco, but he told that to no one. He was not a needful man, but one who was pleased with whatever he made. Because of the dunking, and the slug of strong, clear, medicinal moonshine, the drum beat was disappearing from his head.

Rufus was not a literate man. He was a common mountain man who could neither read nor write, except for his name. He could cipher up to seven; that's how many dogs he had. He had never known schooling, not even a day. He had to run the farm from the age of nine when his daddy died, and he had helped with it before that, but he figured he got by all right without a lot of book learning. He thought common sense was enough. Besides, a very old but learned Cherokee man once told him that education was simply a conditioning of the mind. He had believed the man. His own mind was conditioned to the necessities of the day and the farm. He knew he ran the farm well, and because of his willingness to work as hard as necessary, it produced what he needed, and he and his ma lived a good life, simple but good. They had everything they needed and more. Who could ask for better?

His mother canned a couple of hundred jars of fruits and vegetables each summer and fall, and by growing their own food and canning it for later use, they cut their visits to the store to a minimum. At the store they usually had to purchase only sugar, salt, pepper, baking powder, and a few other things. Rufus dug potatoes, both Irish and sweet, and kept them for the winter in straw-lined mounds of dirt.

They lacked for nothing in foodstuffs.

Unlettered as he was, Rufus was not an ignorant man. He possessed an abundance of common sense. Gifted in the way of true mountain men, he was wise in the use of animals, never once abusing one and allowing no other man to abuse one in his presence. He was an expert woodsman in every respect, and a crack shot with pistol or long gun. He hit what he shot at, and as the sheriff had said many times, Rufus was a good farmer and the best tracker in the county. Many who knew him said he could track a snake over a flat rock and tell what kind of snake it was, but Rufus allowed they exaggerated some. He was able to work when the sheriff needed him. When working as a tracker, he officially carried a gun, but was not on the county payroll. He never wore his badge pinned on his chest, figuring it would be a good mark for somebody to shoot at. It wasn't a sworn deputy's badge, just something to indicate his official standing, if needed. It was always in his pocket, but he had never yet had to show it. He was always armed with a small .32-caliber revolver in his hip pocket. A man never knew when he might need protection.

Rufus wore bibbed overalls, not because they were handier for working around the farm, which they were, but because he hated belts tight around his middle. They caused him gas, which could lead to embarrassing moments. He convinced himself that his body felt freer when his clothing was loose.

The farm was Rufus's pride and joy, especially because he didn't have to work it much. His favorite show-off was a western-type pole corral he had built behind the barn, like those he had seen in California when he and his mother rode the train there to visit his uncle Clyde, who was dying of cancer.

At the moment, his corral harbored only three animals, his female mule, Fred, the cow he called Bessie, and a heavy-hoofed horse for plowing and other farming chores. Rufus had named the horse Bill, in memory of his murdered brother, William. He had plans for running a sizeable herd of horses one day, and eventually would have to enlarge the corral or build another, and clear off the mountainside and grass it. Not a really steep mountainside, it would do well for raising horses and he could also fence off another part and raise purebred cattle, if he wished.

Rufus rode the mule instead of a horse. He thought a mule's gait was smoother, its ride easier, and he always said mules were smarter than horses. They rarely wandered, feeling a comfort and security in the presence of men.

Fred was a fine-boned racing mule, but Rufus hadn't raced her yet in Jackson County. He wanted to wait until the time was right, and that meant when the price was right. Rufus was confident Fred could outrun any horse he had seen run in the county, but he had never let anyone know, not even his closest friends, nor, indeed, his mother, how fast Fred could run. She was a big, powerful mule, a sorrel, generally not tolerant of inquisitive dogs, but to defend herself she could strike out with any hoof in any direction. Beyond that, she could run like the wind.

Like most mountain men, Rufus was tight with his money, although he always carried enough in his pocket to participate when someone dealt the cards or raced horses outside of Sylva on Saturday mornings. He did not put his money in the bank, because he didn't understand banks, but in a metal box hidden in the loft of his house. He had no idea how much money he had. His mother hadn't counted it in a while.

Rufus liked life in the mountains, the helpfulness of neighbors when illness or misfortune struck a family, and the eagerness of fellow farmers to help each other when crops came in, especially tobacco. He wanted his tobacco hung just right in the barn during dry weather, and he tried to do the same when assisting a neighbor.

Slowly he bridled Fred, swung aboard bareback, and rode down the dirt road, headed for town. When he left the farm on the lane that led to a county-kept road, he saw Mrs. Jones hanging out an early morning wash and as he rode by, he doffed his hat and spoke, "Howdy, Mrs. Jones. I saw John Henry on his way up the mountain awhile ago?"

"Yeah, he's a coon huntin' this weekend. How's your ma?"

"Tolerable, I reckon," He passed on by, his long legs swinging his feet below Fred's belly. He never rode a saddle, not knowing when he might get up a race and when he did he didn't intend to burden Fred with the weight of a saddle.

TWO

Autumn of 1917 was beautiful in the mountains of North Carolina. Trees were magnificently colored by every hue known to man, except for black, Rufus thought, and spirits were high even though European war clouds floated over the land. The war had already come to include America. The military draft that June had taken several young men from Jackson, mountain boys like the Hazelton twins, good friends of Rufus's who had joined the army willingly because they relished any kind of fight. As doughboys, they were already fighting in the trenches of France. Rufus himself was of draft age, but had been deferred because of his home situation. He wanted to go to the army, but there was no one else to work the farm and provide for his mother.

Life went on, however, just as it had forever in the hills. All the farmers he knew were coon and fox hunters, considering both recreations to be great sport, sitting on a mountainside before a warm fire, lying like the devil, listening to the music of their dogs running a fox.

"Hear that? That's Ole Buster a'bayin'. Ain't that music to yore ears?"

"Thar goes Big Jim. They must be on the trail of a good'un."

"Yeah. Most likely they'll run all night."

"Most likely."

They settled back to enjoy the chase, spitting tobacco juice in the fire, passing a jug of Rufus's spirits now and then.

"Spirits an' 'backer juice makes a right smart swaller," one of the old hunters allowed.

"Shore do," said another.

"Keeps me up all night," a third chimed in, "with th' runs."

"What's the runs?" a youthful hunter asked.

"Well, jest about ever' thirty or forty minutes, you run to th' little shack out back," said the first old-timer, "an' you either make it 'er ye don't."

The camp rumbled with laughter.

Rufus often joined them, usually taking two of his Red Bones to run with the pack.

On Friday, two days before Rufus's twenty-sixth birthday, four men went into the Balsams on a coon hunt. The following morning, three came out: Fred Palmer, John Henry Jones, and Foley Bumgarner.

Sid Hollifield didn't.

In the sheriff's office in Sylva, the county seat, John Clure walked back and forth, hands behind his back, doing the job he had been elected to do in this high-rimmed Tar Heel paradise tucked in huge valleys between the Great Smoky Mountains and the rugged Balsams. He sat down at his desk, hands pyramided beneath his chin, deep in thought, staring at the wall.

Clure was a big man, tall and discerning, with quick eyes that pronounced intelligence. He wore long dark hair hanging low on the back of his neck, but his killer moustache was showing streaks of gray. On his right side, he carried a holstered forty-five revolver. He said it would stop a charging bull at forty paces.

Suddenly, he looked at his deputy, Larry Gault, and calmly said, “Get Rufus!”

Gault shot him a concerned look. “Raby?” he asked. “Rufus Raby?”

“Get him. . . NOW! Bring him here!” The sheriff's temper began to show.

“What if he’s still drunk?”

“Then douse him in the creek. But bring him. NOW!”

Gault was no genius, else he would have had a better job. Sheriff Clure usually had to tell him twice to do a task, but when Gault did the job he did it well.

Rufus was popular with most of the people in the county, though there were some who looked at him askance because he tended to drink too much and never darkened the church door. There were others who didn’t cotton to him because he minded his own business. Gossip went in one of his ears and directly out the other. He paid no attention to it and refused to take part, which isolated him from those who loved to talk about their neighbors and other acquaintances. They criticized Rufus as being “too stuck up,” but those who knew him well saw how he could do about anything under the sun—and do it well. Too, Sheriff Clure thought well of Rufus, who was a pleasant man when sober, and that counted for something, his friends figured. Drunk, he often looked for trouble and usually found it, but his friendship with the sheriff since the election had kept him walking down the straight and narrow—at least, for the most part.

"Yes, sir," Gault said, moving toward the door, "I'll get him." He had seen the sheriff in a snit many times before and knew that Clure recognized the scope of what the three men in the room were telling him, and nothing about it was good. Clure could sense trouble building.

Gault hurried to the town livery and saddled a horse. Climbing aboard, he headed east at a gallop.

Clure turned to the three, Palmer, Jones, and Bumgarner, and asked, "What the hell went on up there last night?"

"Nothing," Palmer replied. "I mean nothing unusual. Leastwise, nothing happened before we run the dogs."

"Have any liquor with you?"

"We had a jug of Rufus's 'shine," Fred Palmer said, "but we hadn't even pulled the cork. It ain't been pulled yet."

"Start at the beginning," the sheriff said, "and tell me the whole story. A man don't just disappear from the face of the earth. Don't leave nothing out. I want it all. Understand?"

Clure stood, stretching his arms and clenching his fists above his hefty six-foot frame, staring from one to the other of the seated men.

"Talk!" he commanded. "This may be more serious than you think."

In unison they nodded and Palmer spoke first.

"We went in the woods about noon yesterday, about a quarter mile above Rufus's place," he said. "There was me and John Henry and Foley here, and Sid come later. We'd been planning a coon hunt and figured we better go whilst all of us had some time off from work. It had rained the night before but the ground was just damp, and, too, we didn't know when we'd all four be off together again."

"Okay," said the sheriff. "Go ahead."

"We went all the way up Fisher Creek, then switched over and made camp on the west prong of Buff Creek, a good bit below Black Rock, and turned the dogs loose. Pretty soon they got up a coon and we took off."

"All of you?"

"No. Sid stayed behind. The dogs was running uphill and he said he was too tired to run thataway. He'd worked graveyard and didn't feel like runnin' the dogs, so he said he'd get camp set up and start supper if we wasn't back. He was gonna sleep a while first.

"We run that coon a mile or two and the dogs lost the trail at the east fork of Buff Creek, and we never picked it up again, so we come back to camp. We'd been gone three or four hours, I guess, and when we got back, everything was in order, all unpacked and straightened up, only Sid wasn't there. None of his things was there, neither. We knew he was tired and figured he'd just packed up and went home, but that wasn't much like Sid. He loved a good coon hunt and campin' out under the stars, and we was gonna stay two nights."

"He didn't leave a note? Nothing?"

"No," Palmer said. "Nothing."

"Didn't that strike you queer?"

"No, it didn't. He can't write, no how. So we didn't think nothin' about it. We figured he was too tired to hunt and guessed he wanted to sleep in his own bed, so he left. Might'a got lonesome for his wife. She's a pretty thing, you know, 'bout twenty, and built nice where it counts."

"I know all that. Stick to the story."

"Yes, sir! Comin' home, it's all downhill from up there and we figured Sid had just up and lit out. Leastwise, that's what we thought he'd done."

"Any strange tracks around camp?" the sheriff asked.

"We dunno. I guess we left some but didn't think to look. We was some worried about Sid."

"Hmmm," mused the sheriff, scratching his chin. "Don't sound good to me. Something ain't right here!"

"We didn't think much about it till we come out of the woods this mornin'," said Foley Bumgarner. "We went over to Sid's house to make certain he wasn't sick 'er anything, but Sue said he hadn't come home. She hadn't seen him. We asked some of the neighbors and they hadn't seen him, neither, which was a little unusual, so we sent some of the neighbors over to sit with Sue, and come straight on here."

"Sid ain't runnin' round on Sue, is he?" the sheriff asked.

"No, he ain't," Palmer eyed the sheriff closely. "Who'd he run around with? Ain't nobody around prettier than Sue. Nicer, either."

"How old is Sid?"

"He's twenty-four," Foley explained. "Twenty-five come November."

"Somethin' happened to him, Sheriff," John Henry continued. "We ain't got no idea what, but this just ain't like Sid."

"Maybe a painter got him," Foley suggested.

"Ain't been a panther around here in years," scoffed the sheriff. "Besides, a panther wouldn't a'took Sid's things."

"Why, Claude Bryson got follered by one a couple'a months back," Foley interjected, still thinking of panthers. "He went to see Martha Miller up on Fisher Creek and one follered him all the way home. That's four or five mile, from a mile up Fisher Creek to a mile up Buff Creek. He had a .38 in his pocket and when he got in the yard he emptied that gun towards where he thought the painter was, but it wasn't. Then he run in the house and slammed the door and the painter come on the porch and tore three boards off the siding 'fore he went away. Claude said he was the maddest painter he ever saw. Well, he didn't really see it. He heard it thumpin' its tail all the way home from Beta. Ever time Claude stopped to listen, that painter stopped, too, and started thumpin' his tail. When he got in the yard he was afeared that painter would see that he was goin' in th' house an' would charge him. So he jest slung some lead towards that painter and run."

"Tell me exactly where you pitched camp. I want Rufus to get up there and try to pick up a trail right away, or figure something out, anyway," said the sheriff.

"Some people think Rufus ain't all there," Palmer put in, ignoring the question. "They think he ain't all right in the head."

"Well, they're wrong," Clure said. "He's just strange and something of a loner. He's unschooled and a little bit backwards, but he's the damnedest tracker this side of Cherokee, and he's a good thinker, too. He's plenty smart in the woods. He knows them mountains like the back of his hand. Maybe he can find Sid, or at least find what happened to him. If he can't, nobody around here can. You guys beat it now, but come back here at two o'clock. Rufus ought'a be here by then."

The three stood to leave, and the sheriff stopped them. "Wait a minute," he said. "Has Sid been actin' anyway strange, like maybe he had somethin' on his mind?"

"No, not a bit," John Henry said. "Ain't nothin' strange about Sid. He was pretty happy. Reckon he's about the most unstrangest feller I ever knowed."

"No reason why he left camp, huh?" the sheriff asked. "You sure him and his wife get along good?"

"Yeah, they get along real good," John Henry said. "They've had a fight or two, but who ain't?"

"I'm asking you again where you camped." the sheriff said.

"You 'member that old sweet gum tree where Perry Johnson treed that bear?"

Clure shook his head. "I don't," he said, "but Rufus will."

"Right there, under that tree."

"Thanks, men. We'll see what Rufe can find. Stay close to town."

"We'll be over at Velt's Café," Palmer said.

"Good. Set tight."

THREE

"Let's go, Fred," Rufus said to the mule, approaching Sylva. "Quit foolin' around. I'd kinda like to get there sometime today." He spoke to her as if he expected a response. Then he prodded her lightly with his heels and she picked up the pace until Rufus checked her with the reins at the east end of Tannery Flats.

There, a couple of hundred yards away across the railroad tracks and the lumber yard, men were gainfully employed at the tannery. It stunk to high heaven, Rufus thought, with all them putrified cow hides lying in it. Even this far away he could smell the tannery strongly, especially when the wind was blowing this way, but the pay was fair and men who needed jobs could usually find work at the tannery, provided they could stand the stink. They said they got used to the odor after a while and paid it no mind, but Rufus thought they were fooling.

Coming through the flats, Rufus looked at the shacks on the hillside along the road where colored folks lived in terrible conditions. Some worked at the tannery or the lumber yard. One of the shacks, at the top of the hill, was made of tar paper, occupied by an aged Negro man who must've lived a frozen life in wintertime, Rufus thought. He liked the Negro folks and thought the town should put more of them to work, even on menial jobs like shoveling horse manure off the street. Some had no income at all and that didn't strike Rufus right. All were willing to work but couldn't find jobs. Rufus hired some of them to do farm work and had always been satisfied with their work.

Feeling rather jaunty once his hangover wore off, Rufus broke into song as he neared the big curve that would take him to Main Street in Sylva:

My Bonnie lies over the ocean
My Bonnie lies over the sea
My Bonnie lies over the ocean,
Oh bring back my Bonnie to me.

Rufus thought, "I ain't got no Bonnie; never had; never will, I guess." Quickly he looked around and when he still didn't see anybody looking, he sang the second verse:

Oh blow ye the winds o'er the ocean
An' blow ye the winds o'er the sea
Oh blow ye the winds o'er the ocean,
An' bring back my Bonnie to meeeeee.

He hushed just in time. Passing around the curve, Rufus met Deputy Gault, trotting his horse toward him.

"Howdy, Rufe," Larry called out. "That's pretty good singing; you ought to be on the stage, but you'll have to hurry, the last one leaves in ten minutes." He hee-hawed at his own joke.

"Howdy, yourself," Rufus laughed, pulling in his mount. "I been thinkin' 'bout just that," he laughed. "This's the first time I ever sung out of the cornfield. Where you headed?"

"Comin' to get you," said Gault, seriously.

"What for? I ain't done nothin'."

Gault laughed and explained, "Sid Hollifield disappeared in the mountains last night and ain't been seen since. Didn't come home. Sheriff wants you to get up there quick and look for tracks."

"Where at?"

"Back in the Balsams somewhere. Sid went coon huntin' with three other fellers and just disappeared. He ain't come back yet."

"Thought they was gonna spend two nights," Rufus remarked. "Three of 'em come up by my house."

"They was, but the others got scared somethin' bad had happened to Sid and might happen to them, too, so they come on out. Sid's wife said he hadn't been home."

"He ain't got another woman stashed somewhere, has he?" Rufus asked.

"Not that anybody knows," Gault replied. "You ought'a know. You're his best friend. Don't know why he would, considering what he's got at home. Anyway, Sheriff wants you quick as you can get there."

"Relax," Rufus said. "Don't get het up. We ain't a quarter of a mile away. We'll be there in a minute." He kicked the mule a little harder in the ribs and he and Gault trotted into Sylva side by side and pulled up at the sheriff's office.

Clure stepped out to meet them. "That was fast," he said to Gault.

"Met him in Tannery Flats," Gault returned.

"What's goin' on, Sheriff?" Rufus asked.

"Come inside," the sheriff said, and to Gault he said, "Go over to Velt's and bring the others back."

By the time the three reached the sheriff's office, Clure had filled Rufus in on the details known to that point. Foley Bumgarner, John Henry Jones, and Fred Palmer filed in and took the seats they had occupied earlier. Rufus sat on the corner of the sheriff's desk.

"It ain't a'gonna be easy, findin' Sid up there," Rufus said. "Have you ever been up in them mountains, John? Feller could get lost in there and never get found. They're big. Must be six or seven miles to the top, and if I had to guess I'd say they was twenty miles long, east to west, maybe twenty-five. They're awful rough, too. That's a powerful lot of country to look over for a footprint!"

"I don't want just a footprint," Clure replied. "I want a bunch o' tracks. I want a trail. If he's up there by himself for some reason, there has to be tracks. If somebody took him and he's able to walk, he'll leave a lot of tracks. Whatever else he is, Sid ain't dumb."

Palmer interjected, looking at Rufus, "We didn't notice no tracks around camp when we got back from runnin' that first coon. I done told the sheriff we didn't think about looking for tracks. We was plumb too busy worrying about Sid."

"Where 'bouts did you camp?" Rufus asked.

"Right under that there big sweet gum where Perry Johnson treed the bear," John Henry answered, and Rufus nodded.

"Another thing," Rufus said. "What was Sid wearin'?"

"He was wearing his overhauls," said Foley, "and he had a red flannel coat. Be easy to see in the woods this time of year."

"What color shirt?"

"Was brown."

"No," Palmer said, "wasn't brown; it was tan."

"What kinda shoes or boots?"

"He had on them brown clodhoppers of his'n," answered Foley.

"Won't be too hard to find his tracks," Rufus offered, "unless he was carried away. He wears big shoes that make big tracks. His brogans have white soles and a big red star in a red circle on the soles. Won't be too hard to find his trail—if they is one."

"He wears either a twelve or thirteen," John Henry said. "Has trouble finding shoes that fit. Big feet! Big 'uns!"

"I don't know what to think of this, Sheriff," John Henry said. "It could'a been a killin' or kidnappin', but I can't think of a reason why. Sid ain't got no money that I know of. It wasn't a robbery or they would'a gone through all our things, too, but ours wasn't touched."

"I know," Sheriff Clure said. "We can't waste time speculatin', we'll just have to try to find him. You boys go on home and get some rest."

At that moment, a pair of brothers from Addie, Roy and Jack McClure, were on their way to Sylva. They rode a light, one-horse wagon, westward through Beta, a couple of miles east of Sylva. Like always, they turned off the main road to the left, riding past the church and school house and up to Old Field Cemetery to check on the graves of kin buried there. Stopping on a hilltop they surveyed the beauty of the range of the Balsams across the valley toward the north.

"Kinda takes your breath," said Roy.

Word of Sid Hollifield's disappearance had circulated like wild fire through the county.

"Dad blamed if I'd wanna get lost up there," Jack said. "That's a sight of mountains, and with all them creeks and cliffs and valleys and trees, that'd be tough country to get lost in."

Roy agreed. He was fascinated with mountains. "If I got lost up there," he said, "I'd follow the first creek I came to, down the mountains. That'd lead me back to somewhere; then I'd know where I was." He thought a moment and added, "maybe!"

"I wonder," Jack said, "how many deer and bear and possums and coons—and rattlesnakes and copper-heads—we're lookin' at right now?"

"Yeah," Roy answered.

Soon they turned their wagon back to the road and eventually came to Tannery Flats and, a few minutes later to the intersection with the road to Cullowhee that ran alongside the Tuckaseigee River most of the way, and from there they rode into Sylva down Main Street.

FOUR

"Rufe," said the sheriff when his office had cleared out, "we have to mount a search and you gotta lead it. You know them mountains better than anybody around here. I'll stay here at the office and keep a command post till we've found him. I can't climb them hills like I used to, not even a'horseback, but I'll sleep here to be on hand at night if I'm needed."

"No problem," Rufus answered. "I know the mountains like my face in the mirror. We'll need good men. A lot of 'em if we're gonna cover the whole shebang."

"We'll get the men. We'll cover from North Fork east of where they camped, to the Indian Reservation to the west," Clure said, "and I'm gonna get some of the Cherokees to search the woods there."

"Let's start now," Rufus suggested.

Jack and Roy McClure rolled up to the Sylva Supply and climbed out of their wagon just as Rufus and Clure emerged from the Sheriff's office. Jack looked diagonally across the street and saw the sheriff, standing before the jail, waving at him. When he waved back, the sheriff beckoned him and his brother over.

"Boys, we've got a problem on our hands," the sheriff said, and both Roy and Jack nodded.

"We know," said Roy. "We've heard about it."

"We need help and you boys can give us a hand."

"Name it," Jack said. "We got all day. We just rode to town to see what's goin' on."

"Figured I could count on you two," Clure said. "Here's what I want you to do. We need men who know the mountains and are capable of climbing them, if need be. We have to search the Balsams from Black Rock to Cherokee. You ride back to Addie and round up men we can depend on, and sweep up what you can around Beta; in fact, get everybody you know from here to Addie—even to Willits, Cope Creek, Blanton's Branch, Buff Creek, Ochre Hill, North Fork, everywhere."

"We can do that," Jack said. "When do you want 'em?"

"Now. Quick as they can get here. We gotta get men in the woods today and start lookin' before Sid has a chance to get out, or somebody who took him has a chance to slip him outta the country, or find him if he's layin' up there hurt," and the sheriff added reluctantly, "...or dead."

"How many do you want?"

"Many as we can get," the sheriff replied. "Tell 'em to report to my office. We'll give 'em their areas to search when they get here."

"Shore enough," Jack said. "We'll get you a bunch. This'll be right down their alley. We ain't had nothing like this in a long time."

"Okay," said the sheriff. "Thanks, boys, and get going. Be sure to tell everybody you get that they may have to spend a night or two in the woods. They'll need to bring their blankets and something to eat, and tell 'em to come armed. No tellin' what we may find up there. And," the sheriff added, "tell some of them to bring their dogs and all of 'em to bring a horse, if they can. It's tough walking up in them hills. If the dogs can get a scent, we'll be in business. We're gonna be spread out from North Fork to the Indian Reservation."

As the two walked back toward their wagon, Gault came up.

The sheriff said to him, "I saw Preacher Dietz drive up. He's over at Velt's drinkin' coffee. See if he'll take you to Cherokee. We want Osley Big Bird, Charlie and Joseph Walkingstick, Fred Chiltoskie, Butch Saunooke, and Sam Goingback. Tell 'em to find somebody over there with a truck or a fast wagon and team and get 'em here as quick as they can."

The sheriff could think of no reason Sid would disappear on his own. He was married to a beautiful woman, had a good-paying job, and a nice home on the eastern edge of town.

Clure had no doubt that hunting parties large enough to comb all of this side of the Balsams could be formed. These mountaineers responded in numbers quickly to any need.

It had been a while since the town had had a crisis of any sort and this one had the feeling of a big one. Clure searched his memory and could not remember a single disappearance that promised the magnitude of this one—at least not in his two terms as sheriff.

Of course, the Balsams were of such ruggedness that any man who had no more experience in the woods than Sid could find himself lost almost as quickly as the bat of an eye.

With enough experienced woodsmen searching the forests, Clure had no doubt that Sid would be found, that is, if bad luck had not befallen him. There were places in the Balsams, he had been told, where a man could fall over a cliff or down a waterfall and not be found for weeks, if at all.

A feeling of dread was beginning to come over him and he wished that enough searchers would show up quickly.

The streets were beginning to fill with people, most of them coming to see what was going on.

"Maybe we can get some searchers outa this crowd," the sheriff said.

Clyde Rector walked across the street to join the men in front of the sheriff's office.

"What can I do to help?" Clyde asked. He had been a rugged athlete at Sylva High School and could skin up the mountains as well as any man.

"Lot of people in town," said the sheriff. "Go up and down the street, Clyde, and round up all you think are capable of climbing the mountains. We need as many good hands on this as we can get. They may have to camp out tonight, so tell 'em to come fixed and armed. If a man has a horse or can borrow one, tell him to bring it."

"Gotcha," Clyde responded and started up the street.

"Now you and me'll get down to business, Rufe," the sheriff said. "Come on in. I got maps of the Balsams tacked on the walls. I want you to divide the area into sections and give a section to each squad of men we get."

"Where's Buff Creek at?" Rufus asked first, needing a starting point. When Clure pointed to it, Rufus knew where he was. "This here's Fisher Creek, I reckon."

"That's right," said the sheriff.

Rufus, unable to read the map, nevertheless knew the territory. Clure helped him when he was stuck on a mountain or a stream.

"All right, here's the way I want 'em spread out," Rufus said. "I'll get some of the boys and scout the area from Fisher Creek to North Fork and up the mountain to Black Rock. That's a prime area, 'specially because that's where he was—or should have been—when this problem rose.

"We'll need a bunch to search Hornbuckle Creek to Shut-In Branch, but tell 'em not to go on the Indian reservation. Then put some in to look all over the woods from Beta to Rocky Face. Eight or ten'll do there. He might'a gone thataway. I doubt it. That's a small area. We'll need another bunch to look from Jenkins' Ridge south to Dills Creek, and that's a lot of country. Put twenty men or more in that gang, if you can get 'em. As others come, assign them to areas. The more the better.

"That'll cover the area pretty good. If we think we may need to go over the mountain and search the Maggie side, we can do that when we come to it."

"Okay," said the sheriff, who had been making notes.

"I'll pick squad leaders who can choose their men and we'll get crackin'."

"While we're waiting for 'em," Rufus suggested, "me and you better go over to Sid's house and get something from Sid's things to give the dogs a scent."

"No need," said the sheriff, looking out the window. "Here comes Sue now."

They met her at the door and brought her in. She carried an unwashed shirt of Sid's. Her eyes were red from crying.

Sue's a beautiful woman, Rufus thought. She didn't take a seat, but stood in full womanhood, her dress clean and pressed, her long dark hair flowing down her back, her body slim and shapely and perfectly erect. Sometimes she wore her hair in a bun, but today it was loose, which Rufus liked better. Her dark brown eyes looked the room over as if she were searching for something. Her face was heavenly shaped, Rufus considered, and the thought almost took his breath away.

All in all, she was the prettiest woman in the county, if you asked him. But he had no designs on her. She was a friend. Today she might be a newly widowed friend and he was filled with pity for her, partially because Sid and Sue had been his best friends. He thought it unusual that she could look so good and so well under the burden she presently bore.

"I thought you'd need something of Sid's for the dogs to get a scent," she said. "Here's an old shirt I haven't washed. It should give them all the scent they need."

"Thanks, Sue," the sheriff said. "We'll need it. Mind if we tear it up and give pieces to each group of searchers? And don't worry, we'll find him. We'll have the woods full of men by mid-afternoon."

"Please do find him, Sheriff. I just know he's alive. He may be lying somewhere up there injured and needing help, and you can do what you want with that shirt. It's an old one, anyway."

She turned to leave. The sheriff hesitated a moment, then asked, "Sue, is there any reason he wouldn't want to come home?"

"No, Sheriff, no reason at all," she said. "Believe me, he'd come home if he could. Find him—please!"

They watched her walk out and up the street.

"Boy!" Rufus exclaimed, "she's as purty as a speckled pup! Seems like yesterday she was a little pig-tailed girl a'runnin' around. She's too purty a woman to let go to waste."

"Yeah," the sheriff chuckled, giving Rufus a sharp look. "A woman gets growed up all of a sudden." Rufus was still watching her walk up the street, a faint smile in his eyes. "I shore hope we can find Sid for her."

In twenty minutes a crowd began to gather at the sheriff's office, all with coats and blankets, rifles and food, and a few dogs. Their horses were tied at the hitching rails.

An hour later, men began to drift in from Addie and vicinity. They, too, were equipped for camping and had food in their bedrolls. A dozen carried rifles or hand guns.

Eddie Sutton, like Rector a great athlete, arrived from

Cullowhee. "Thought you'd need a hand," he said to the sheriff.

Sheriff Clure was pleased. "That's quick work, men," he said to the crowd. "There's already about forty of you. Did everybody come ready to spend a night or two in the woods?"

They shouted yes and knew the hunt was soon to begin.

"Okay," yelled the sheriff. "We'll split into squads and take off." He named Clyde Rector, Andy Blanton, and Eddie Sutton squad leaders and broke the men into squads numbering as many as Rufus told him to.

By noon, seventy armed men stood around the sheriff's office, all eager to get in the woods and on with the job. More were coming, they said.

"We'll send 'em in the woods as they come in," the sheriff said.

"What about the Indians?" someone shouted.

"We'll tell 'em to search the reservation when they get here."

"Put Osley Big Bird in charge," Rufus said.

"Yeah," returned the sheriff, "my mind's been runnin' thataway."

Minutes later, Clyde Rector and Andy Blanton didn't answer the call for squad leaders. Then, neither did Eddie Sutton.

"Where are they?" asked the sheriff.

"They went thataway," someone answered, pointing to the east. "Went with Rufus."

"All right," the sheriff said, "then I want Clyde Bumgarner, Bob Shuler, and Pos Stevens for squad leaders."

Meanwhile, with Preacher Dietz at the wheel, Gault neared the Cherokee Indian Reservation in a brand new Model T Ford.

The preacher was talkative.

"Bought this car the other day," he said. "Liked it so much, I don't ever 'spect to buy another one. At my age, I figured two cars would do me the rest of my life, so I bought another one like this one and put it in my garage. It's jacked up on blocks and we took the tires off and put them up to keep them from rotting.

"Now, if I wreck this one, or if something else happens to it," he added, "I'll have a new one to drive."

He sped as fast as the rutted road would allow and when they reached Cherokee, the men they sought were handy, loafing about the settlement, all but Saunooke.

When Gault explained the situation, Big Bird said, "I know Sid. Good man. Give us time to get our things together and we'll get to looking in the woods on the east side of the reservation. If there are any tracks coming on the reservation, we'll find them."

Lisa Silver®

FIVE

When the crowd of men swelled, Sheriff Clure shouted, "Boys, we're a'dealin' with something here that we don't know much about. Only thing we know is that one of our good citizens is missin', lost in the woods. We've got to find him, dead or alive, and let's pray he's alive.

"You've already divided into squads. Rufus has left to check out the campsite. Maybe he can come up with something we can use.

"Now, let me tell you this. John Henry said nothing of the other three's things was bothered, so it wasn't a robbery." He had their full attention. "Has to be that somebody's took him or he's hurt and wandering, or laying up in them mountains somewhere with a broke leg or a snake bite and likely don't know where he is.

"When you get in the woods, work in pairs for safety, look close and be careful not to trample any tracks. Call out for him now and then. Measure any big footprints you find. Sid wears a big shoe with a star on the sole. You can't miss his tracks.

"You ought to ride your horses, but watch the trail ahead so you won't miss or mess up any tracks. Look sharp. This is important. If you do see something suspicious, send word to Rufus and he'll check it out. He'll be over around the headwaters of Buff and Fisher Creeks.

"Sid might'a strayed off the trail, but that's hard going, so look sharp around you, and especially at the trails. Study them. We don't want to miss a track."

The sheriff thought for a moment. "Likely he's on a trail goin' somewhere, but he don't know the woods. He's never spent much time in 'em. That's against him and against us in our search, so we have to notice everything. Look for anything, like snapped twigs or trampled weeds or broke bushes, and especially tracks.

"If somebody took him, you might find a lot of tracks on the trail. If so, look for a big track with a star in it."

The sheriff paused briefly and looked around. Every eye was on him, every ear cocked, listening intently to his words.

"Question anybody you meet," he continued. "Find out what they're doing, take down their names and where they're from. Ask if they've seen anybody or anything that might be suspicious. Ask 'em about any tracks they've seen, 'specially them with a star in 'em.

"Check out any place a body could be hid. If you see a place that's been freshly dug out that could hide a body, see what the dirt has been dug for. Dig anywhere the dirt's been disturbed."

"Sheriff," someone asked from the crowd, "what'll we dig with? We ain't got no shovels."

"Dig with a stick. Use your hands," the sheriff replied so all could hear. "Pay no attention to a couple'a broken fingernails. Just dig!"

"What'll we do if we find something?" another asked.

"If you find something suspicious, fire three shots in the air with a heavy rifle.

"Our parties will be spread out so far it might be hard for all of 'em to hear, so if you're a long way off and hear three shots from another area, fire three more to alert anybody that's too far away to hear the first ones. Then all of you beat it to the place where your leader is. When he's satisfied that everybody's with him, head for the place where the first shots were fired. But if some are farther out than you are, wait for 'em and all of you go together to whoever fired first. We don't want to leave nobody in the mountains.

"Now, all of you won't be together in your quadrants; you'll be scattered, but squad leaders, don't scatter your men too far apart, and work 'em in pairs. Sweep back and forth across your quadrant, movin' toward the top of the mountain. And all of you men be careful. Don't get trigger-happy. Don't shoot each other. Don't shoot nobody. These ain't posses, they're huntin' parties."

The sheriff paused and looked over the crowd.

When he got everyone's attention again, he concluded, "If you hear four shots, come on off the mountain. We'll have found him. Remember, if you find him, fire four shots.

"Now, that's all I've got to say, but remember every word I told you. We need to find Sid, and find him quick. This is the best way me and Rufus could think to find him. Squad leaders, count your men. When you leave the woods, make sure all of your men come back.

"Any questions?"

"Yeah, I got one," someone in the back of the crowd raised

his hand. "Them mountains is pretty rough, some of 'em jest about straight up and down. I ain't sure I can climb anything like that. I ain't sure nobody here can climb some of 'em.

"Why, some of 'em's as steep as Court House Hill yonder," he gestured toward the court house which sat upon an extremely steep hill. Ninety-nine concrete steps had been built from the street up to the court house at the top.

"I couldn't climb nothin' like that," the fellow said. "Ain't nobody here could climb that. Why it's purt near perpeduclar."

"Purpee what?" the sheriff asked.

"Straight up," the man answered.

Toward the front of the crowd, two other great athletes, Forrest Bryson and Jim Ryan grinned at each other and nodded their heads.

They took off down the street like scalded cats, hit Court House Hill at a run and ran all the way to the top.

The sheriff laughed.

The man turned to Clure and said, "Great gobs of goose-flesh! They clumb that'air hill like two big jackrabbits!"

No one else questioned the steepness of the mountains they faced.

"Good luck, boys, and God be with you. Go get him!" said the sheriff.

The crowd turned away and formed in squads upon their leaders, and that way they rode out of town, heading for the wilds of the Balsams.

These were tough men who had grown up in the mountains, spent time running ridges, knew every trail, every spring, every rock cliff, and most of the caves. Clure thought he couldn't have found better men for the job.

Some, who had cooked off a few runs of moonshine were welcomed to the search. They knew every place a man could be hidden. The sheriff was satisfied with them, and he knew more were coming. He held Ferris Bryson back to lead those who came into the hunt later.

By nightfall, there were more than a hundred men searching the woods from North Fork to the Indian reservation.

Lissa Silver©

SIX

Meanwhile, Rufus's group, all four of them, arrived at the sweet gum tree on Buff Creek's west fork. Rufus stopped his men a hundred yards short of the tree.

"You boys tie yore hosses tight to a couple of them trees," he said to Clyde Rector, Andy Blanton, and Eddie Sutton, after he tied Fred to a sapling. "I'll have a look around. You stay here. Too many of us might spoil something important."

He rolled a cigarette and put a match to it. "Have a cigarette, boys; I'll be back directly."

Sutton said, "Rufus, you know we don't smoke."

"Then have a beer—on me."

"Where? Ain't any beer up here."

"Then piss in the creek an' take a nap. This may take a while. I ain't a'goin' out of sight," Rufus said. "I can't rush this, boys. I'll be up there under that old sweet gum."

He started toward the campsite, stopped and turned, "Tell you what. Give your dog a sniff of that shirt, Andy, and all of you take a turn around the camp. Keep out as far as you are now and circle the campsite. Look good along the creek. Don't tramp on no tracks. Look for anything, tracks, broke branches, rocks turned over, anything. If you find somethin', holler."

They spread out and began to cover the ground closely,

peering at every object. Immediately west of the campsite, they came upon a track. "Hey, Rufe," Andy yelled. "Here's a track."

Rufus came over and studied the track. It was a large one, but without a star.

"Hmmm," Rufus pondered, "that's a big'un. Maybe a size twelve. How many feet that size do you guys know of around here?"

"I never pay attention to the size of feet," Clyde Rector said, "but we could check the shoe stores in town. Maybe Sol Shulman would know."

"Good idea," Rufus said. "Measure that one and write it down, then go on out thataway where it's pointed." With his chin he pointed west. "But don't go out of sight. Take the dog."

Back in camp, Rufus bent over to study the ground again, still soft from the recent rain. There were bare spots and upon one of those Rufus found one of Sid's tracks with the big, two-inch star on the sole, and there were many others, tracks on top of tracks, probably made by the other three campers, or else those who took Sid away, and Rufus could distinguish nothing about them that would lend itself to intruders.

"That's strange," he said to himself.

He bent closer to the ground and studied the tracks. Some had been obliterated.

"Hmmm," he mused, half aloud. "This ain't too many tracks. Four men in camp, counting Sid, make a lot of tracks."

He searched closely around the camp and found other tracks, but none that could be identified.

"Hey, Rufe," Ed Sutton yelled from a hundred yards out. "Come here a minute and look at what we found."

Rufus walked to where the three men stood staring at the ground.

"That's the biggest dadjimmed cat track I've ever seen," Andy said.

Rufus bent over and studied the track.

"What's goin' on here?" he asked. "I ain't never seen no cat track that big. Have you measured it?"

Yeah," said Ed Sutton, "It's eight inches wide and seven and a half long."

"Lord have mercy!" Rufus exclaimed. "That cat must be as big as a cow! And look at them claw marks."

Rector said, "I ain't believing what I'm lookin' at."

"He's headin' west," Rufus said. "Come on, boys, Let's see if we can trail 'im. Spread out about eight or ten feet apart and watch where you step. Look for big shoe tracks, too, and watch out for snakes. Give your dog another sniff of that shirt, Andy." The four moved slowly along, but after a quarter-mile they had found no more tracks. The dog had detected no scent, either at the campsite or beyond.

"I didn't find nothing' helpful in camp, either," Rufus said, "except that one track of Sid's and them of the other campers. You boys finish your circle of the camp. See if you find any more cat tracks, or big shoe tracks, and then let's get back to town and see if anybody else has found anything and come in."

They found several tracks a hundred yards on out, but not any of a big shoe and no cat tracks.

"Could'a been anybody," Rufus said after studying the tracks. He pondered a thought for a minute. "Them tracks is a coupl'a days old. Before we go back," he said, "Let's go farther west and see if we come up with anything else."

They walked almost a mile but turned up no tracks of the cat or of a man wearing big shoes. Distantly, down the mountain, they could hear voices of other searchers calling back and forth, and Rufus knew the search was thorough.

"Look here," said Ed Sutton, walking over to the left of the others. "Here's one of Sid's tracks. See that big star?"

Indeed it was, firmly planted in a soft spot of earth, and it was pointed north.

"Wonder why we didn't see any more before this?" Sutton asked.

"I know that's strange, but keep goin', boys," Rufus said. "We may be onto somethin', or it's possible they're carryin' Sid.

After another quarter mile, nothing else was found.

"Tell you what," said Rufus, "Let's scout up the mountain a ways and then work back towards camp. Search ever' step. Don't miss nothin'."

Up the mountain, they turned east toward camp and suddenly came upon another cat track, fainter on the ground, but its size matched the first one.

"No question about it," Rufus said. "It was made by the same cat, an' it's goin' east. But where are the rest of his tracks? Come on. Let's look some more."

They continued on, rifles at the ready, and two hundred yards farther, Andy exclaimed, "Look here!" He pointed to one of Sid's tracks. "Look at that star!"

"Well, I'll be dad blasted!" Rufus exclaimed. "Why would they be comin' back thisaway. That track's pointin' towards the east." He thought a minute, then said, "Andy, you come with me. You other two keep lookin' up and down, east and west. This here's startin' to be a puzzle. Camp here tonight, but not in their camp. We'll send up some more men to help you search the area tomorrow. When they get here, start 'em north towards Black Rock, but tell 'em to stop this side of the rock. I'm goin' up there myself tomorrow and I don't want to have to separate no tracks."

He walked back to camp where Andy waited. Up the hill, he saw Rector and Sutton moving along, studying the ground carefully.

"Come on," Rufus said to Andy, "let's get goin'."

Andy's dog, though trailing all the way, had not picked up a scent.

"Strange," Rufus commented to himself. "Mighty strange."

Lissy Silver©

SEVEN

Before Rufus and Andy left the woods for Sylva, Rufus thought a moment, then shouted to Rector and Sutton, "While you still got some daylight, why don't you spend the rest of today lookin' around on the east side of Buff Creek? Look up and down the creek. I don't remember checkin' that side. Then if you don't find nothin' there you might go on out a little ways to the east, cut up the mountain for maybe a half mile. After that, come back and camp here somewheres.

"You better stay up here till new men come. I'm gonna send about twenty more up here and tell 'em to find you two. You spread 'em out and have 'em search up towards Black Rock, but make sure they stop short of the rock. I'm goin' up there tomorrow and search the ridgeline myself from North Fork to the reservation. Tell 'em to be shore and don't go to the top. I don't want 'em messin' up anything I might find up there."

Rufus reported to the sheriff, "Send twenty men up Fisher Creek and on over to Buff Creek tomorrow mornin' and Rector and Sutton will tell 'em what to do. If nobody's found anything by tomorrow night, call 'em all out of the woods. I think the hottest clues must be in our area, an' maybe we can do somethin' with 'em, but I've got to get some rest if I'm goin' back all the way to the top. I'm gonna sleep in my own bed tonight and go back up tomorrow.

"In the morning, I'm a'goin' to the top and look around. No, I don't want nobody with me. Just me, myself, an' I. That's three of us," he jested. "That's all I want. I wanna see for myself if I can find anything on the ridgeline. Ma always said too many cooks spoil the broth, and I reckon she was right. I'm gonna look from North Fork by Waterrock Knob and Black Rock, all the way to the reservation, an' I might even go in there a piece, right along the spine of the mountains. When I finish I'll come out and see you and we'll decide what to do next. Might be we'll cross the mountain and look down the Maggie side."

"That's fine with me, Rufe," said the sheriff. "Don't wear yourself out. We got other men who can search, too."

"Yeah, but most of 'em couldn't foller a trail through a plowed field," Rufus responded, and the sheriff laughed.

"Just don't try to do too much," said the sheriff. He paused a moment, thinking. "You think he's dead?" he asked Rufus.

"Likely," Rufus replied. "If he ain't, with so many men lookin' for him, we'll either find him or sign of him. I can't understand it. Don't make no sense to me, so few tracks up where they camped."

Rufus's mother fed him well that night and early the following morning he was up and ready to go.

First, he dug into an old duffle bag and came up with a pair of strong field glasses. Then he rolled up a heavy coat, put on wool socks and his boots. He made sure his pistol was among his gear, that it was loaded, and extra ammunition was included. He also took a .30-30 Winchester rifle.

After breakfast he put the bridle on Fred, climbed aboard, and left, heading up Fisher Creek. Then just as dawn was breaking, he cut over to Buff Creek.

Presently he came to the camp of Rector and Sutton and they were waiting for him.

"Find anything?" Rufus added.

"Yeah," Sutton said, "coupl'a things that might mean something."

Rector tossed one of Sid's shoes to Rufus. "Found that on the other side of the creek," he said. "And we've got another little surprise for you. We went to every one of Sid's tracks that we found the day before yesterday and all of 'em were made with that shoe. No right-footed tracks in the bunch. Don't that strike you a little odd? Then Ed went to all the cat tracks we found and every one was made with the same paw. That's a little queer, too."

"Ah huh!" Rufus exclaimed. "That don't sound good, does it? Maybe we got something here, but I ain't got the least idea what."

"Come over to the creek, we want to show you something else. We found a pretty good trail of two or three men going down the creek.

They led Rufus to a sandy bar on the east side of the creek that contained tracks going downstream.

"Three of 'em," Rufus said. "'Peers to me somebody's playin' games with us."

"Here's the big one." Sutton said, "but there isn't a star in it. It's three or four sizes bigger than the others."

Rufus studied the track. "What's different about them tracks there?" Rufus asked.

"Big ones are deeper," Sutton said.

"Wha'zat tell you?'

"He's a big man."

"Or?"

"He's carrying something heavy."

"Like a body, maybe?" Rufus asked.

"Yeah," Sutton responded. "Could'a been Sid. What did he weigh? About a hundred and sixty? One big man could carry him."

"Notice anything else?" Rufus asked.

"No."

"Why do you think they went south?"

Rector said, "To throw us off."

"That's right," Rufus answered. "They would'a turned north, but started south to make us think that's where they was headed."

"I believe it," Sutton agreed.

"All right," Rufus responded, "I'm a'goin' to the top and look around. Don't want nobody up there with me. Rector, you and Sutton foller this trail down the creek. See where it goes west, or it may turn east, but if it goes west, then get to Sylva as soon as you can and send word to Osley Bird to be on a sharp lookout. If this trail turns east an' then north towards Black Rock, mark the place and you go on out."

"Mark it with what?" Sutton asked.

"You got a hatchet there. Chop a mark in a tree beside the trail to Black Rock, an' then go on out. I'll find the mark. I'm gonna stay up here a day or two and see what I can find. Don't want nobody with me. Besides, most are out of the woods by now. They've had time to search their areas three times and if they don't find him in three tries, they might as well go home."

Actually, by then all the searchers had left the woods.

"You're gonna stay up here?" Rector asked.

"Yeah. Gonna see what I can find on top of the mountains."

"They might'a gone over toward Hornbuckle Creek," Rector said.

"I ain't much thinkin' thataway," Rufus said. "But I'm gonna look around Black Rock first an' then search along the spine of the mountains west toward the Indian Reservation."

On second thought, Rufus added, "One'a you stay here. If you hear me fire four shots, I've found him. You fire four more for somebody below to hear and spread the word. Then you come on up after me and leave somebody there to bring up anybody who comes up from Sylva later. Bring 'em up the mountain and you'll find me up there somewheres.

"Ever'body know what I want you to do?"

They answered "yes" and left.

When they headed for Sylva, Rufus donned the heavy coat, knowing the air would be colder on the ridgelines. He made his way to the top of the mountain and went east until he came to Waterrock Knob, a sheltered place good for camping. There he fed Fred, tied her for the night, made a camp for himself, lit a small fire in the lee of an outcrop, and ate a cold supper from his pack.

The fact that he found no tracks on the trail—no recent ones, at any rate—told him that the murderers had avoided the trail, if they had come that way at all. The thought occurred that he would have to look farther down the mountainside to find any tracks or other clues to the route the killers had used to dispose of Sid's body.

It also entered his mind that Sid's body might never be found. There were a hundred places in the hills where a body could be hidden and possibly never found.

EIGHT

The disappearance of Sid Hollifield had a decided effect on all of Jackson County. When outside their homes, folks kept a watch all around, fearing they knew not what. At night, they began locking up the house, all the windows and all the doors, something only a few had been accustomed to doing before. They watched all children playing outside, and called all of them into the house before dark. Now, with something mysterious lurking about, if they didn't have door locks, they rode or walked to Sylva and bought them at the hardware.

By the second night following Sid's disappearance almost every home in the county was locked tight. If a neighbor knocked on a door after dark, no one opened the door until identity was established. Only when he got a favorable response did the man of the house unlock the door and let the neighbor in.

Rufus was up with the dawn. Clouds had sprinkled a bit of rain, and he found himself hoping it would stop, else it might wash out any tracks on the mountaintop, if, indeed, there were any, which he was beginning to doubt.

He ate a hurried breakfast, then climbed on Fred and began riding toward the west. Rufus had only gone about a quarter of a mile when he suddenly hauled back on the rein and stopped Fred.

"Whoa, girl," he exclaimed. "Maybe we're goin' the wrong way." He looked to the rear, back toward the east. "Think we'll go back and look in the other direction first. We ain't looked around North Fork yet. Let's go take a look there." It was the west prong of North Fork, heading up east of Waterrock Knob.

The trail leading from Waterrock Knob eastward to the headwaters of North Fork was precipitous. Along the trail were bare, gray, granite rocks. Once, the granite hovered over the trail like a shelter, forcing Rufus to bend over and lay his head alongside Fred's neck. Stunted trees dotted the passageway, dead more often than not, blasted by lightning. In the trail were fallen trees that Rufus had to climb over, leading Fred, to continue the path he followed.

He stopped to breathe lungsful of fresh mountain air blowing in from the east. "Breathin' this air," Rufus said to Fred, "is kinda like drinkin' cold spring water."

A touch of fall was in the air, too. Rufus felt a chill in the wind. He looked south into the distance and clouds were dark and menacing and advancing toward him. "Looks like we might get to go swimmin' without jumpin' in the creek, Fred," Rufus said.

He had not yet reached North Fork when the storm struck. Rufus turned Fred back to the shelter of granite over the trail, dismounted, sought the driest spot he could find, built a fire with wood each camper left in the shelter, and settled down to watch the storm.

Huge bolts of lightening lit the surroundings, and occasionally he heard an explosion, then the ripping noise of falling trees or rocks where lightening struck, and huge blasts of thunder assaulted his eardrums. He was forced to wait a dismal half-hour for the storm to pass on over Maggie Valley down the mountain to the north.

"Dang it, Fred," Rufus said when they moved onto the trail again, "that washed out any tracks we could'a found; you can bet on that. I'm glad none of them lightening bolts hit that shelter we was under."

He cut down North Fork, rounding Yellow Face on the east, and came to a knoll that offered a good view of the creek for a long distance.

There he dismounted, took the binoculars, and began to study the creek, its banks, and off both sides for a short distance out.

He saw nothing unusual, just another creek flowing from the top of the Balsams that might have passed for any other stream in the mountain range.

His attention was suddenly drawn to a tangle of brush a half mile down the creek, and a few yards east of the water. The brush was perhaps ten feet wide and fifteen or twenty feet long. In the center of the tangle was what appeared to be a hump. Thinking it probably was a large rock, he slowly gazed on down the creek, then came back to the tangle.

Nothing strange about it, Rufus thought, simply a bunch of blackberry vines and other brush around it, yet every time he thought to turn away, something seemed to pull him back.

"Hmmm," he finally mused aloud. "Somethin' 'bout that don't seem just right"

He looked carefully along the creek beyond the tangle, and studied the creek up the mountain to a hundred yards from where he sat, but he saw no similar tangles. Then he widened his vision and studied the area twenty yards to both sides of the creek, and still nothing like the tangle appeared.

Very carefully then, he searched the area around the place with his binoculars.

"Could that be a bear's den?" he asked himself, and a few moments later answered, "Could be, I guess."

He saw nothing further that interested him, so he turned back to Fred, put away the field glasses, and mounted.

"Let's go back to the other side of Waterrock Knob," he said to the mule, but after a few steps, he stopped Fred and looked back down the mountain. There was, indeed, something intriguing about the brush but he couldn't understand what it was. He had a hunch, nothing more, simply a hunch, that he ought to go down and check out that clump of brush.

"Well, Fred," he said, "we ain't got nothin' but time on our hands. Let's play our hunch and go see what that brush pile really is. That 'air hump might be where somebody hid his still."

They threaded their way down along the headwaters of North Fork. Soon they came to the brushy place on their right. He saw immediately that a part of the tangle was blackberry vines, most of their leaves gone. He looked for tracks but any there might have been would have been washed away by the storm.

Moving on around toward the front, he noted that the hump had an opening. "A cave!" he exclaimed.

"C'mon, Fred," he said. "Let's go look at it closer."

There was still nothing unusual about it when Rufus dismounted twenty yards from the cave. From there he thought he could see a trail going through the brush.

"Bear's den," he said in dismissal, and started to re-mount. Then he looked at the place again and said, "Let's take a better look."

He tied Fred to a small tree and made his way toward the brush. Approaching the cave, he heard the dry rattle of a snake. Casting his gaze about, he found a rattlesnake to his right, so he stepped to his left and immediately a snake hit its rattles there.

Backing away, he reconnoitered to find a place where he might see more clearly into the cave, and finding a place, he peered again and saw something white near the front of the cave opening.

"Odd!" he said. "Don't look like no rock."

He walked back to Fred, pulled the field glasses out of the sack, and returning to the spot from which he had seen the white, he focused the glasses, and immediately his view of the white blob became a white sole of a shoe on which was a circle of red with a two-inch red star inside the ring.

"Huh oh!" he exclaimed, "That's Sid's other shoe," but he could make out nothing else within the darkness of the cave.

He relocated the snakes and killed both, then he tried to approach the cave along the overgrown trail leading toward it, and suddenly the brush around him resounded like a whole singing convention of rattlesnakes shaking their tails.

Turning, he went back to Fred, took his Winchester and facing down the mountain at an angle to his right, he fired four fast shots in the air. Moments later, sounding distant but clearly reports from a rifle barrel, he heard four answering shots.

He rode Fred back to the crest of the ridge, turned west and made his way back to Waterrock Knob.

There he sat down to wait.

NINE

Rufus built a fire, for the air was cold. The first contingent of men to arrive included Clyde Rector, Andy Blanton, and Ed Sutton, Bobby Jones, Bob and Bill Shuler, Max Blanton, and Bill Sutton.

Shortly after noon, forty men sat around smoking cigarettes and drinking coffee, talking in hushed tones. Rufus told them only where and how he had found the cave, that he had almost left without seeing what the clump of brush was, and that in the darkness of the cave he could only see the sole of Sid's shoe. He also said there were many rattlesnakes in the den. How many he couldn't guess, only that he heard enough rattling to scare him away. Don't want no truck with rattlesnakes." He said.

"That's about it, I guess," Rufus said, rising to his feet. "Somebody leave a note for anybody who comes later, telling them where we are. Let's get goin' and see what we can do about getting rid of them snakes.

"By the way," he added, "how many of you got shotguns?"

Ten hands went up. James Lee Blanton said, "I've got a double barrel. Does that make eleven?"

"I guess so," Rufus laughed, "if you can you hit anything with it."

"It's always hit where I point it," James Lee returned.

They tied their horses to brush around the knob from

which Rufus had first spied the brush pile and headed for the pile on foot.

"Keep your distance," Rufus ordered when they arrived at the brush. "We got to figure out how to get them snakes out'a that den an' kill 'em so's we can get to Sid's body."

Several other men rode up before someone said, "Let's cut away the brush."

"It's full o' snakes," Rufus said. "I see nobody's wearing high boots, and I know I ain't a'goin' in there till we get rid of them rattlers."

"Wish we had old Bill Johnson up here. He'd know how to get rid of rattlers," someone spoke up.

Suddenly Rufus began to laugh. He said, "This ain't no time for jokes but it just come to mind," he said, "about a poker game Bill Johnson had one night at his cabin way up on Buff Creek.

"Some of his friends had come up and played all night. Sometime after midnight they heard a rattler rattlin' out in the yard and somebody says to Bill that he ought to go out an' kill it. He did, and when he come back in somebody asked how big that snake was and Bill said he didn't know, but from the feel of it, it was a big one. The first feller asked why he didn't go out and find it and pull the rattles off its tail so's they could see how old it was.

"He did. Bill went out and got down on hands and knees, pattin' the ground till he found th' snake, and jerked the rattles off its tail. They was seventeen rattles an' a button on it, and somebody allowed it must have been a big'un.

"Next mornin' when the game broke up and the boys

got ready to leave, they went out in the yard and found the snake Bill had killed a'layin' there with the rattles still on his tail."

Laughter rolled around the crowd. Bobby Jones spoke up, "If we can't cut the brush, we'll have to burn it? The wind's at our back. It'll blow smoke into the cave and smoke 'em out."

"What about Sid?" Bob Shuler asked. "If we burn the brush, it might catch him on fire."

"We ain't got no choice," Rufus said. "Gimme all you shotgunners on a front line here. Some of you good rifle shooters stand off to the sides an' if snakes come out towards you, kill 'em."

Cutting a small sapling, they bundled dried sage on its end, tied it tight, and Bill Sutton lit it. The flames caught slowly, then spread, making a good fire. Rufus and Ted Mull pushed it into the brush, which caught immediately and began to smoke. The wind carried smoke into the cave and set off a furious rattling among the maddened snakes.

Suddenly a shotgun boomed and a rattler flipped and rolled the last of its life from its body. Then the shotgunning became a cacophony and snakes died in their tracks. Off to both sides rifles boomed as rattlers tried to circle the fire and get away.

"Okay!" Rufus shouted. "Let 'er die down 'fore it gets in the cave and gets at Sid."

The flames diminished into a thick smoke, which flowed into the cave and brought out more rattlers.

"Must'a been a hundred in there," Rufus said. "Let the fire die down the rest of the way, but kill any more snakes that come out."

As the smoke diminished, the brush lay in smoldering ashes and a couple of men began to stomp snakes immobilized but not killed by the shotgun blasts. Some of the searchers pulled pint bottles from their overall pockets and passed them.

Soon, the cave appeared to be empty of snakes and three men advanced to enter it.

"Hold on, there," Rufus commanded. "Wait up a minute." He picked up a rock and flung it in the cave and the rattling began again.

"Stay out'a there," Rufus said. "Throw a few more rocks in and maybe that'll bring some more out."

A half-dozen rocks were heaved in and rattlers began to slither out of the cave again. Gunfire stopped them just outside the cave.

After a couple of minutes, Rufus called a halt to the shooting and said, "Throw some more rocks in."

Several were thrown, but no more rattling came from the interior of the cave. "All right, men," Rufus called. "Go ahead and stomp some more snakes. Make sure they're all dead. We don't want to have to carry no snakebites out'a the woods today."

Several men clubbed the live snakes to death until no more appeared to be living.

"C'mon now," Rufus said loudly. "But ever'body take your time. Be sure a snake's dead before you step on or over it. And watch out when we get to the body; there may be snakes under it."

Sid's feet lay at the opening of the cave, and his body was entirely inside.

"Wonder how they got him in there?" Roy McClure asked. "With that many snakes in the pit, looks like we ought'a have some dead men around here. You know some of 'em must'a got snake bit."

"I dunno," Rufus answered. "Okay, couple of you get a'hold of his feet and drag him out. Slow now."

That way, Sid's body was removed from the cave. All over his face and hands were fang marks where he had been struck by rattlers.

Rufus had never experienced such a feeling, not even when his brother was killed, as he watched Sid's body removed from the small cave. A tear rolled out of one eye, and then another from the other eye. This was the best friend he ever had, and to see him in such a condition and think of how he was killed almost overwhelmed him.

Beneath his breath, Rufus told himself that he would never feel whole again until he found Sid's killer.

"I devote my life to that," he said to himself. "I'll never rest till I've found the ones responsible for this. I promise that to you, Sid. I'll find them if it takes twenty years."

Rufus looked around the cave and saw a round object against the back of the cave.

"What's that over there?" Rufus nodded his head toward the object.

Jack McClure eased over and discovered it was Sid's bedroll. He brought it out. "We can give this to Sid's wife," he said.

"Wait a minute," Rufus said. "There's somethin' else over there in the corner?"

"Looks like a broom," someone said, probing the darkness of the cave.

Rufus scuttled across the floor and came back with a big stuffed and sewn cat's paw tied on half a broom stick.

"Well, this answers our questions about that big cat," Rufus offered, and the others nodded.

"I sure hope he was dead when they put him in there," Eddie Sutton added. "Can't imagine a worse way to die than in a rattlesnake den."

Sid's body was lifted out of the brush and placed alongside the trail. Looking at his friend lying there with snakebites all over his hands and face, a deep feeling of loneliness gripped Rufus. Finally he turned away and ran his thoughts to other things. His grief was almost overpowering.

"Now," Rufus said, "some of you burn the rest of that brush and see if you can stomp the top of the cave in. I'd rather not have a den that big right here beside the trail. Somebody might come along who ain't as careful as we are."

A half-hour's work burned the remainder of the brush, and the bodies of the rattlers were thrown in the flames. Then ten minutes of stomping by heavy men brought the roof of the cave down. With small limbs cut by hatchet from nearby trees, the sides of the opening were caved in and the earth smoothed over. No sign of a rattlesnake den remained.

"Anybody make a count of snakes?" Rufus asked.

"I counted over thirty," someone said.

Another spoke up, "I stopped counting at forty-five."

Men shivered at the thought of Sid being pushed into that snake den alive.

"Let's make a stretcher of some kind," Rufus said, "and get Sid on out and down to Doc Hooper's. He might be able to tell us if he died from snake bites."

All told, it was late in the afternoon when the crew was ready to move. Rufus said, "Let's try to get to the Fisher Creek road before dark. From there we won't have no trouble in the dark."

That they did, with several men helping the heavy drinkers and others trading off on the stretcher handles, and by ten o'clock, Rufus knocked on Doc Hooper's door. The doctor answered the door in his nightgown, and when he saw the burden the crowd bore, he pushed back the door and said, "Bring him on in."

Half an hour later, Doc Hooper came outside and announced to the waiting men. "Them snakes was chewin' on a dead man. Sid was killed by a blow to the back of his head with some kind of heavy instrument."

"Like maybe a rifle butt?" Max Blanton ventured.

"Yeah," the doctor answered, "like maybe a rifle butt. He was hit from behind and never knew what hit him. Busted his skull wide open. He doesn't have any swelling from snakebite because he was already dead."

"Let's take him on over to the funeral parlor," Rufus said, "an' see if they can cover up some of them fang marks before Sue sees him."

"Wait a minute," Dr. Hooper said, "there's something else. He was shot through the heart at close range. There's powder burns on his shirt."

"Shot?" Rufus exclaimed. "He was shot?"

"Through the heart," Dr. Hooper said.

"Can you tell which killed him?" Rufus asked. "Was it the blow on the head or the shot?"

"Oh, he died from the blow on the back of his head," Dr. Hooper said. "There was no blood from the bullet wound. He was already dead when he was shot."

"Whoa!" Rufus exclaimed. "Maybe we can get something to go on from the shot. Can you dig the bullet out, Doctor?"

"Yes," Dr. Hooper responded. "That was easy. I've already probed it out and here it is."

He handed Rufus a lead bullet.

"Hmmm," Rufus mused, studying the bullet. "Thirty caliber, I'd say."

He passed the bullet around the crowd and most of them nodded that it was, indeed, from a .30 caliber rifle.

"We'll give it to the sheriff," Rufus said. "He'll know what to do with it."

Sid Frady handed the bullet back to Rufus, who examined it and put it in his overalls pocket.

"Did anybody search his pockets," someone asked.

Nobody answered.

"Doctor," Rufus asked, "would you see what's in his pockets?"

The doctor went back inside and returned in a couple of minutes. "They're all empty," he said. "Nothing in them at all.

"Thanks, Doctor," Rufus said, and the crowd began moving away. Bob Shuler and Ted Mull carried the stretcher.

"Who's gonna tell Sue?" Forrest Bryson asked. "I'd hate to have that job. She sure loved this man."

Sheriff Clure, who had just joined the crowd, spoke up. "I think Rufus ought'a tell her. He found Sid and he knows Sue better than any of us, and he's got an easy way with words. Will you do it, Rufe?"

"Reckon so," Rufus said. "I'll have to think up a way to tell her easy like."

"If anybody can do that," the sheriff said, "you can. It's your job, Rufe, but was I you, I'd wait till morning. Likely she's abed by now."

Lissa Silver©

TEN

Gingerly, Rufus knocked on Sue's door at ten o'clock the next morning. Nettie Jones, wife of John Henry Jones answered the door.

"Come on in, Rufus," she said. "Sue's still asleep. I s'pect you've come to tell her about Sid. I been sitting up all night and I'll just go on home. When she wakes up, be easy with her. She's pretty tore up. He is dead, isn't he?"

"He's dead," Rufus answered. "I'll be easy, Mrs. Jones."

Nettie got her coat and left. Rufus sat before the remains of a fire in the fireplace trying to think what he would say to Sue. He tumbled words in his mind, trying to find the easiest way to tell Sue that her husband was dead. He had never before been faced with that dilemma, and he couldn't even think of a way to start.

Next thing he knew, he woke in Sue's rocking chair. Fully dressed, she had watched him sleep for half an hour, then gently shook his shoulder and asked, "Rufus, what have you come to tell me? Sid is dead, isn't he?"

Rubbing sleep and fatigue from his eyes, Rufus said, "Sue, it ain't good news. We found him, an' he's dead, all right. He's over at the funeral parlor now."

"How did he die?" she asked.

"He was hit over the head," Rufus said, truthfully. He figured he should give her what details he could without upsetting her too much. "We don't know who did it, but you can bet we'll find 'em. An' when we do, killin'll be too good for 'em."

He still said nothing about the snakes or the rifle bullet. He told her only that he had found Sid's body in a cave beside North Fork Creek and that he had been killed before he was put in the cave. "Least," he said, "that's what Doc Hooper told us."

Seeing that she was about to break up, Rufus stood, and with tears rolling down her cheeks, Sue stood, too.

She buried her face in Rufus's chest and cried.

He didn't know what to do, so he gently put his arms around her and held her close and let her cry. "I'm sorry, Sue. Go ahead and cry. It's all right. It'll do you good."

Finally, her crying slowed to sobs and then ceased. She looked up at him and, wiping tears from her eyes, said, "Oh, Rufus, I'm glad it was you who came to tell me and that you're here now. You're just like family, and you were Sid's best friend. You're a good man, Rufus, and a nice man. Would you like some coffee?"

"Reckon I would," he said, "but you set down and I'll make it. You just set there and cry all you can. Get it out of your system."

He could hear her weeping softly as he made coffee in the kitchen over a fire Sue had built when she got up.

Soon, he returned with two steaming cups and gave one to her.

"I'm going to miss him terribly, Rufus," she said. "I came from the head of Buff Creek to marry him, and he was my hero and my teacher, and such a great part of my life."

"I know he was. He was as good a man as I ever knowed," Rufus said. "Maybe somebody'll come along after a while that pleases you as much." He paused, knowing he had said the wrong thing and trying to find something with which to cover it.

"Me an' my big mouth," he blurted. "I ort' not be talkin' to you thataway right now."

"It's all right, Rufus," she said. "It's all right. I know what you mean. I'm still glad it's you and not someone else, or some crowd, who came to tell me."

He quickly finished his coffee and made ready to leave. "Will you be all right, Sue?"

They stepped out on the porch.

"Yes, I'll try to sleep some more. I imagine some of the women will be along soon."

"Yes."

"Thank you for being so kind, Rufus." She leaned forward and kissed him gently on the cheek, and he sensed the warmth of her body. His consciousness of her womanhood giddied his head and set his brain to whirling. He had never before had such a feeling, never scented a woman before. Never had one kissed him! A surge of euphoria burst in his soul and shot through his veins.

She was profoundly grateful. She had kissed him out of gratitude. They both knew that.

He had no idea what was happening to him and felt he must get away at once.

She extended her hand to him. "Thank you again, Rufus."

He shook her hand and suddenly his breath shortened and he turned quickly from her, missed the top step and fell headlong down the porch steps."

"Rufus!" she exclaimed. "Rufus! Are you hurt?"

"No," he said quickly, scrambling to his feet, his face red as a beet.

"Wasn't watchin' where I was goin'." A warmth he did not understand rose in his head.

"Are you sure you're all right?" she asked.

"Sue," he looked into her eyes. "I reckon I'm about the all-rightest feller in the county long 'bout now."

He didn't realize why he felt that way, nor had he any idea why he had said that. The words had simply burst from his mouth. He told himself that he was out of his head, that his brain was not in working order.

Knowing nothing else to do, he fled, bounded onto Fred's back, and together they hit the road at a gallop.

Bad news or not, Sue began to laugh at Rufus's riotous departure.

ELEVEN

Rufus isolated himself on the farm for two days. With nothing else to do, he cooked off a run of mountain dew.

No trail led to the still, which was totally hidden from sight of anyone who entered the dense woods along Possum Branch and passed by the knoll on which the still sat. Huge oak trees surrounded the knoll, sheltering it with long branches that dissipated all smoke from the fire.

All sorts of brambles surrounded the knoll, growing thickly on its sides. Anyone who approached the still had to make his way through the thorny blackberry bushes and other assorted brambles.

Rufus approached the still in a different way every time he came to work it, thereby making no trail that could be followed.

Sheriff Clure had seen the still and one day watched as Rufus cooked off a run. His visit was "purely educational," he said, for he had never seen a distillery in business, and he was not a drinker. He marveled at the operation, and realized he was watching a master distiller at work.

On the day of Sid's funeral, Rufus's mother rode to the church in the wagon with John Henry and Nettie Jones. Shortly afterward, Rufus rode Fred to town, tied her down the road from the church, and went inside just as the service began. He sat on the back row.

He could see Sue, and she was weeping, but not loudly. The pallbearers sat to one side. Rufus looked at them with no malice, but with the thought that Sue had requested him to be one. He was still so embarrassed, he had thought of a reason to decline.

Just before the end of the service, Rufus slipped out of the church quietly, mounted Fred, and rode home.

The next day Rufus trotted Fred back to Sylva. He entered on Back Street and rode up toward the cemetery. To his right was an untended field filled with beautiful fall flowers.

He hauled Fred to a stop, slipped off his back, and with a pocket knife, cut a fistful of flowers, tied them with a piece of cord he carried in his pocket, then rode on to the cemetery, placed them on Sid's grave, and sat on a rock to the side and thought about Sid.

Rufus knew he would miss him, though the thought had not struck him hard since he found the body. He recalled the good times he and Sid had spent together. Once they even drove to Asheville in Sid's daddy's big Cadillac automobile, bouncing over rough roads, but they enjoyed seeing the city and the large number of people on the streets, and, of course, all the big buildings—some of them six stories tall—and other sights. They were two big-eyed country boys come to town.

For an hour Rufus sat lost in thought, and when he stood to leave, a voice behind him said softly, "Rufus."

He recognized Sue's voice and slowly turned to face her. She was alone.

"I thought I would come and tell Sid goodbye once more." A tear rolled out of her eye, and she turned and wiped the tear away.

"I'm sorry," she said.

"Don't be," he said. "Ever'body knows how much you and Sid loved each other. If you want to cry, cry."

"I'm all right. I'm glad to see you," she said. "I didn't see you at the funeral."

"I was there," he said, toeing the ground, eyes downcast toward his feet. "I sat in the back of the church and left just before it was over."

"Why?" she asked, "and why haven't you been around to see me this week? I thought you might come."

"No," he said.

"Why not?"

"Well," he said truthfully, "I guess I was a little embarrassed 'bout the way I left you the last time. Reckon I made a fool out of myself."

"No, Rufus," she said. "You didn't make a fool of yourself. I was happy you were there, happy that it was you, Sid's best friend and the one who found his body, rather than someone else. It wasn't foolish the way you left. But it was rather funny." They both laughed.

"Guess it was, at that," he said.

"It was," she answered.

Suddenly, Rufus felt perfectly at ease, able to talk with her about this and that, and enjoying her company.

When they stood to leave, he asked, "How'd you get up here?"

"I walked," she said.

"Well, can I walk back down the hill with you?"

"Of course, you can," she said. "If you're hungry, we can go over to my house and I'll fix supper."

"Can't do that," he said. "Half the town'll be there."

"No, not tonight," she said; "that was last night. Some of the women have been there this afternoon, making excuses why I wasn't home. I just needed to get away for a while and walk around."

"Well," he suddenly got his nerve up, "if you're hungry, let's go down to Velt's Café and eat a bite. That'll be all right. We'll be where ever'body can see us all the time. Won't give nobody nothin' to talk about."

"Yes," she said, smiling. "Let's do that."

They whiled away an hour in the café, and a few people came by to tell Sue how sorry they were. In the end, he led Fred down the street by the bridle and walked Sue home, where he bade her good night and climbed on Fred's back more slowly than the last time he left there. He chuckled, thinking about it, and from the porch he heard Sue laugh. She was thinking of it, too.

Rufus saw Sue infrequently that winter, and just a few times did he talk with her. He and Sheriff Clure were busy trying to get a handle on who killed Sid, and there were no clues—at least, none they could find so far.

He spent the remainder of the winter just working

around the farm where there seemed to be a million things to do.

The weather was bitterly cold. Several more Jackson County boys were drafted and by spring most would be fighting, and perhaps dying, Rufus thought, in France, wherever that was.

At first, Rufus wished he had been accepted by the army—he loved a good fight as well as anyone. But when he thought of his poor mother living alone, trying to work the farm, he was glad to still be home where he belonged. After all, his mother came ahead of France!

Fighting and dying didn't scare him. He scarcely thought about it. He was young and full of beans and, uneducated as he was, didn't know much about war—until two Jackson County friends of his came home from the army in boxes. One was buried at Balsam toward Asheville, and the other at Savannah, southwest of Sylva.

He began to think about the war then. He also gave thought to the competition to his whiskey business, because the search for Sid had turned up eleven hidden whiskey distilleries scattered through the Balsams, but no one had said anything about them to Sheriff Clure. They weren't hunting stills, they reckoned; they were hunting Sid Hollifield.

Larry Gault resigned from the deputy's job in December, saying that since his brother had died in October, he had to go home to Cullowhee Creek and tend the family farm.

"Hate to see you go," said Sheriff Clure. "You've been a good deputy, but I understand that family comes first. So, good luck, and drop in to see us whenever you're in town."

"I'll do that," Larry said, handing the sheriff his badge.

"Oh, before you go, there's one more thing I want you to do."

"What's that?"

"Get Rufus!"

Rufus was sworn in as deputy sheriff later that day, and Clure told him his salary would be the same as Gault's, eight dollars a week.

"That ain't much," Rufus said, "especially since a man might have to put his life on the line to uphold the law."

"That's a starting salary," Clure said. "Do a good job and you'll make more money."

"All right, I will," Rufus said. "Now, give me something to do."

"Go out on the street," the sheriff said with a twinkle in his eye, "and preserve the peace."

Rufus chuckled.

"And pin that badge on your shirt. People need to know you're the law, now. Don't keep it in your pocket like you did the other one."

Rufus pinned the star on as ordered and was still chuckling as he closed the door behind him.

Sue spent most of the winter at home by the fire, seldom alone, reading and working around the house.

Neighbors dropped in almost every day. She hired a teenaged boy to cut her firewood until late February when Rufus found out. He walked into her back yard the next day and told the wood chopper, "Go home, I'm takin' over this job an' do it right."

"But she hired me," the boy said.

"Git!" Rufus said gruffly. He handed the boy two dollar bills as he left. "Gosh!" the boy exclaimed. "Thanks, Rufus."

When Sue heard the chopping going much faster, she went outside to check, and saw Rufus swinging the ax. She was pleased and said she would go right in and cook supper and Rufus knew she was a good hand at cooking.

That evening, Rufus and Sue shared dinner in her dining room.

Next morning the whole town knew about their supper at Sue's.

A late winter snow fell softly, but didn't lay as Rufus came to town about noon to talk with Sheriff Clure. Before they started trying again to figure out the mystery of Sid Hollifield's murder, Clure looked him in the eye and said, "Rufe, the whole town's talking about you and Sue."

"That so?" Rufus was surprised. "What are they saying?"

"Well, they seem to like the two of you getting together," Clure answered, and Rufus felt he was blushing from his boot tops up. Then the sheriff added, "Anything going on that shouldn't be?"

Rufus looked him in the eye. "No, they ain't! If anybody's sayin' different, tell me about it. And there ain't no match! We've always been good friends, Sid an' Sue an' me."

"Nobody's saying anything bad," the sheriff answered, "except a couple of the Hannessey boys."

"Ah huh!" Rufus exclaimed. "What they sayin'?"

"I won't repeat it," Clure said, "but they are over at Velt's right now."

"All right," said Rufus quietly, squeezing his right fist into his left palm. "John, I'll be back in a minute."

Out the door he went, his face as clouded as the sky, and, as the sheriff watched, Rufus pulled off his badge and put it in his pocket and almost ran to the café.

Charlie and Pete Hannessey sat at the counter. Neither paid attention to his entrance.

Rufus stopped behind them.

"Git up!" he demanded loudly. "I said git up!"

He jerked Pete around and his big left fist smashed him in the mouth, knocking him backward off the stool to the floor. Blood splashed on the counter.

Charlie stood to protest, "Now, see here..." and Rufus hit him in the stomach with such right-handed force that he was lifted upward over the counter and fell to the floor behind it. Rufus's fists were big and he put all of his two hundred pounds of force behind the blows.

Charlie came up and Rufus smashed him in the mouth. Blood spouted a second time on the counter and he went down and didn't come up again.

Rufus jerked Pete toward him, his fist drawn back for another blow, and Pete crumpled to the floor, holding one hand over his smashed mouth and the other stretched toward Rufus in supplication.

"We didn't mean nothin' by it," Pete spluttered, blood flowing from his mouth. "We was just joking."

"You're a liar!" Rufus exclaimed. He dragged Charlie from behind the counter and shoved him to the floor beside his brother.

Shaking a finger in their faces, Rufus shouted, "If I ever hear of you two, or your brother, sayin' anything 'bout Sue and me, I'll kill you. You hear me? I'll kill you dead!"

He turned and stalked out, the entire lunch crowd staring at him, applauding silently in their minds.

Rufus left the Hannessey brothers lying on the floor, hands over their mouths. He went across the street licking his bruised knuckles.

"What happened?" the sheriff asked.

"Nothin'," Rufus snapped.

Clure looked out the window across the street and saw the Hannesseys emerge from the café holding their mouths with blood dripping between their fingers, and he looked at Rufus sucking his knuckles and laughed. "Better start carrying your pistol." Rufus withdrew the .32 Special from his overalls pocket and showed it to the sheriff. "I'm carryin' it," he said.

"You're my full-time deputy now, Rufe," Clure said. "You're officially on the payroll. Get a belt and holster and wear the gun in sight. And pin on your badge."

"Gun gets in the way of farmin'," Rufus said.

"Then carry it in your pocket when you're farming, but you could get in action quicker from a holster."

"Don't think I'll have to," Rufus responded. "Them Hannessey boys don't wear no holsters."

"Bet they will next time you see them, and they'll be gunning for you," Clure said. "If they make any move toward a gun, kill 'em in self defense."

"I ain't gonna shoot nobody down less he goes for his gun first," Rufus growled.

"Then get a holster and belt," the sheriff said, "and beat 'em to the draw and tell 'em to stick 'em up! That's an order. And while you're at it, swap that pea-shooter for a forty-five and learn to shoot it. That's an order, too."

TWELVE

The next morning, Rufus entered the Sylva Hardware. The store was empty except for Joe Samples, who owned and operated it.

"Howdy, Rufus," Samples said. "What can I do for you?"

"Need a gun," Rufus said.

"Rifle? Pistol? What?"

"Pistol. Forty-five caliber."

"That's a big one," Samples said. "Don't get many requests for them. Is it for you?"

"Yeah, it's for me," Rufus answered. "Sheriff thinks I need a bigger gun. Told me to get a forty-five and a holster, too. He's carryin' one hisself since Sid got killed."

"You want a new or used one?"

"I don't give a hoot, Joe; he just said to get a good forty-five an' learn to shoot it."

"Well, lemme show you what I've got," Joe led the way to the firearms section at the rear of his store and Rufus marveled at the long rack of rifles and the glass cases filled with handguns.

"Sell a lot of guns around here, don't you?" Rufus commented.

Joe withdrew a pistol from the case and handed it to Rufus. "It's used," he said, "but ain't a finer handgun in the store."

"What kind is it?" Rufus asked, hefting the pistol and liking the balance and feel of it.

"It's a Colt Peacemaker," Joe said. "Thirty, forty years ago 'most everybody in the West carried one. They say it's the gun that won the West."

"Is it that old?" Rufus asked.

"Don't know how old it is," Joe responded. "A stranger come in last week and said he wanted to swap me a good pistol for a rifle. He might not a'knowed what he had, but I did. I figure I got the best of the deal and he got the rifle he wanted."

"Need a holster, too," Rufus said.

"Here's the one he traded me," said Joe, pulling a holster and ammunition belt from the case. "It's hand-tooled and has twenty-four loops for carryin' shells. You'll notice the holster fits on the left side on the front of your hip bone, makin' the butt tilt towards your right hand. That's fer a quick crossdraw. Like old Wyatt Earp and Hopalong Cassidy and them other cowboys used to do." He laughed and Rufus grinned.

"How old do you reckon it is?" Rufus asked.

"No idea," said the shopkeeper. "Might be thirty, forty years old. But it's in good shape. I took it apart myself an' cleaned an' oiled it and fired it some, and there ain't a thing wrong with it. Probably been laying up or hanging on the wall for years. It ain't been used much. It has a seven-and-a-half-inch barrel that's been re-bored. When it come out it was a forty-four caliber but somebody re-bored it for a forty-five. If you have any trouble with it, bring it back and I'll take a look at it."

Rufus liked the feel of the gun, and he liked the walnut grips, making the pistol less showy than pearl or ivory handles.

"I like it. I think I'll take it," Rufus answered. "How much?"

"Nothin'," said the proprietor. "You're buyin' it for your work. I'll bill the county. Taxpayers'll pay for it."

"Well, that's good," Rufus said. "How 'bout some cartridges."

Joe laid three boxes of shells on the counter. "That'll hold you a while," he said.

"Hope so," Rufus said, "but I'm gonna have to learn to shoot it."

"Maybe you ought to take a couple more boxes."

"Yeah, lemme have 'em, and bag this stuff up. Don't want ever'body in town seein' it just yet."

"You got plenty o' space to practice on that mountain," Joe said. "Get a big old oak and blow it full o' holes. An' you might practice quick-drawin' a little bit, cowboy. Never know when you'll have to get in action mighty quick."

"I'll do that," Rufus laughed, and carried his load out the door, adding as he went, "but I ain't no cowboy."

"That's no reason you can't learn to shoot," Joe yelled after him.

Next morning, Rufus dressed as usual in bibbed overalls, came downstairs and strapped on his new firearm. His mother watched him.

"Got ye'self a new gun, I see," his mother said.

“Sheriff wanted me to carry a forty-five,” Rufus answered.

“Mighty big gun. Your pa never had no pistol. He always used a rifle.”

“I know,” Rufus said, buckling the filled cartridge belt in place.

He walked around the room, and the belt slipped off his slender hips and he caught it before it reached his knees.

“Hmmmm,” Rufus hummed. He tightened the belt a notch, the pistol snug to his left side, butt pointing across his body.

Three steps later, it slid down again. He wrestled with himself, trying to keep the gun in place.

“Somethin’ wrong with this holster,” he said. “Can’t keep it up.”

“It ain’t the holster,” his ma said. “It’s you and them overhauls. That gun’s heavy and you’re so skinny in the hips you ain’t got hips enough to keep it up, not with them overhauls on. You ain’t got much of a waist to help it stay up.”

“Well, I’ve got to figure a way,” he said.

“Don’t have to figure nothin’,” she said. “What you’ll have to do is go to town and buy you some pants an’ shirts an’ learn to wear ’em.”

“Pants an’ shirts?” he questioned. “I ain’t wore nothin’ but overhauls my whole life.”

“I know,” she said, “but if you expect to wear that gun and hold it up, them overhauls is too straight to keep it up. Besides, it’s time you learned to dress decent.”

"I can't do that, Ma. Maybe I can haul it around in my pocket."

"Maybe so," she said, "but it's heavy and it might slip down when you need it most. Pants and shirt'll solve your problem. You better go on an' get 'em."

"Aw, Ma, they must be some way."

"No way," she shook her head. "Go on, now. Get you some new britches. You ought to anyway. You ain't no farmer no more an' ever'body knows it. You're a deputy sheriff. You need to look like a deputy sheriff, not a farmer. Besides that, folks is a'talkin' about you and Sue. If you're gonna court her, you can't court her in overhauls, not these days."

"Reckon you're right," he capitulated before all of her words registered, and, red of face again, he said, "I'll go now. Back in a coupl'a hours."

She eyed him sharply and began to smile.

Trotting Fred into town, Rufus said aloud, "Reckon I'll go see Sol Shulman. He'll know what I need."

He stopped in front of Shulman's Department Store, dropped Fred's reins to the ground, knowing the mule wouldn't move out of her tracks while he was in the store.

Shulman himself greeted Rufus as he walked in. "Hello, Rufus, what can I do for you?"

"Reckon I need some pants an' shirts," Rufus answered, "an' maybe some boots."

"Heard you'd been made a deputy," Shulman said. "Congratulations!"

"Don't know whether to thank you or not," Rufus answered. "Maybe you better wait a few days to congratulate me. I ain't been in no ruckus yet."

"I imagine it won't take you long to cure that," Shulman answered. "It never has!" He was a nice, friendly man who clothed half of Jackson County.

He measured Rufus's waist and his leg length and began shuffling through stacks of pants on the tables.

"You might be tough to fit," Shulman said. "Let me give you some of different sizes to try on and you go back in that little room where the curtains are and see which ones fit."

"This ain't my idea, Mister Shulman," Rufus said, "but I can't keep my gun up on my side when I buckle it around my overhauls. It keeps slidin' down towards my knees."

"I think this will cure that," Shulman said, and Rufus headed for the dressing room.

When he returned he was smiling. "I think we've hit on something," he said. "These pants feel good. Fit good, too." He had on a pair of gray whipcord trousers and a dark blue shirt with his deputy's badge pinned on his chest and the forty-five buckled on his hip.

"You look good," Shulman said after inspecting Rufus for the fit. "They do fit well. I'm sure Sue will like them, too."

Dad blame it, Rufus thought, but he ignored it and said, "Better let me have about three pairs an' make 'em different colors. An' a coupl'a belts."

"Coming up," said Shulman, choosing Rufus's trousers from the rack. "You know, Rufus, if you have trouble with your belt being too tight, you might think of suspenders."

"I'll see," Rufus said. "Never thought suspenders looked good, 'cept on fat men. How much do I owe you?"

"You don't owe me anything," Shulman replied. "I will bill this to the county. It's the same as buying uniforms."

"Well, that's right neighborly of you," Rufus said. "That's what Joe told me over at the hardware when I got a new pistol."

Shulman replied, "Nothing neighborly about it. Just the way we handle things with the county."

"Thanks," Rufus said, taking the package and turning to leave. Suddenly he stopped, turned back to Shulman and asked softly so no one else could hear, "How many men around here do you know with big feet—like size twelve or better?"

"Well, let me see," Shulman studied the floor, letting his thoughts roll over those who were his customers. "William Goodson of Cherokee, Sid Frady of Addie, Pete Wilson and John Watson here in town, and Jerome Bryson at Cullowhee. They come to mind right off. Goodson's got the biggest feet. He wears thirteens."

"Anybody else?"

"I'll have to study on it," Shulman answered. "Might be some more."

"I know it ain't them," Rufus offered, "but the man who killed Sid Hollifield was wearin' big shoes. Least, all the tracks I found was big."

"I'll let you know if I think of any more."

"Fine, and thanks," Rufus said. "These pants feel pretty good, an' my holster ain't slippin' down a bit."

As he stepped out the door of Shulman's emporium, Rufus bumped headlong into a large man, and backing off, said, "Sorry 'bout that."

"It's all right, Rufe," said the man. Peering closely at him, Rufus exclaimed, "Well, if it ain't Robert Queen! Thought you was in the state of Washington, gettin' rich."

"Was," Queen said. "Working in the timber fields an' will be again soon as I spend a few days with my ma."

"When did you get in?"

"Come in yesterday on the train. Sorry to hear about Sid. He was a good fellow. Too bad, coming to your end in a rattlesnake den."

"He come to his end before he was put in the den," Rufus said. "Thank God!"

"Got any clues?" Queen asked. "Anybody you're looking at?"

"Nope," Rufus answered, "nobody. We ain't even found one clue yet."

"Well, it's too bad about him and 'specially about Sue," Queen said, matter of factly. "But he left her pretty well fixed—for a few weeks, at least."

"Pretty well fixed?" Rufus asked. "What you talkin' about?"

"About the money he won the night he died," Queen said, "or maybe it was the night before. I wasn't there; wasn't in town yet."

"What money?" Rufus asked.

"The six hundred dollars he won in a poker game at Clyde Preston's house," Queen said.

"Six hundred dollars!" Rufus was amazed. "Awful high stakes game, wasn't it."

"Thought so," Queen said. "I wasn't there. Bumped into Clyde yesterday and he told me about it. He said Sid had the dad-gumdest run of luck he ever saw in a game of cards. I'm glad he had it, though; six hundred dollars'll take Sue a long way."

"Thanks, Robert," Rufus said. "I gotta get back to work. I'm late already."

He hurried down the street and crossed over to the sheriff's office at a trot.

Rufus burst in the door so quickly Sheriff Clure came out of his seat behind the desk. "What th' heck?" he asked. "Hey, you look pretty good, dressed up that way. And I see that the holster'll stay up on them pants. You're rigged just right for a quick draw."

"Quit yer kiddin' an' listen to me," Rufus said. "I maybe found a clue to Sid's murder."

"Clue? What clue?"

"Sid won six hundred dollars in a poker game at Clyde Preston's house the night before he went coon huntin'. Take me more'n eighteen months to make that much."

"What?" the sheriff exclaimed. "Why haven't we heard this before now?"

"Well, I ain't seen none of them that played in the game," Rufus said.

Clure was visibly upset. "Get going," he said. "Go to Clyde and confirm it and then see if he left the money with

Sue. And don't worry too much about your own money. You'll get a raise and a bonus if you crack this case."

"I ain't never worried 'bout money, an' I'm on my way," Rufus said, and hurried out the door.

THIRTEEN

At the livery stable, Rufus put his arm around Fred's neck and rubbed her nose, and swore that Fred smiled. He pulled the halter into place and jumped aboard, reining out of the livery and up the street to the east at a fast trot."

Three miles out of town, he crossed the Tuckaseigee River Bridge and pulled up at Clyde Preston's home, dropping the reins to the ground.

He rapped on Preston's door and Amelia, Clyde's wife, answered. "Why, Rufus," she said, "it's good to see you. Say," she looked him up and down, "what happened to your overalls?"

"Couldn't get my pistol to stay up on my waist," he said. "I had to get me some pants to hold it up."

She looked at the big forty-five in Rufus's holster. "Looks like you're ready for bear."

"Don't know 'bout that," he answered. "Is Clyde at home?"

"Yes," she said. "Come on in. I'll get him. He's out back chopping wood."

In moments Clyde, a large, muscular fellow with gray hair and a big smile, entered the room, shook hands warmly with Rufus and allowed, "Heard you took Gault's place. Good move for Clure."

"Don't know 'bout that," Rufus answered, "but I'm here

on business. I heard that Sid Hollifield won six hundred dollars in a poker game here the night before he disappeared. That so?"

"Yeah," Clyde returned, "it's so. Never saw such a run of luck in my life. Seems like he filled about every hand."

"That's a lot of money. Were you in the game?"

"No, I wasn't. Too steep for me. I ain't seen six hundred dollars in a year or two."

"Neither had Sid," Rufus returned. "What time did he leave?"

"Before eleven. He had to work graveyard."

"Anybody object to his quittin' the game?"

"Naw, nobody. They was right glad to get rid of him."

"Who else was here?" Rufus asked. "Who else knew he won the money?"

"Well, Clayton Evans from Franklin, Sam Mayberry and Ben Johnson from here, Lon Phillips from Cullowhee and Dan Souther from Whittier played a few hands and when they saw the way Sid's luck was runnin', they dropped out and watched the rest of the way. And then there was Samson Reed from Balsam. He lost about fifty dollars and then quit, but what he lost was about two weeks pay for him. He works at a restaurant in Waynesville. Makes about twenty or twenty-five dollars a week. And Tom Hannessey."

"The Hannessey boy stayed?" Rufus asked. "He played all the way? How much did he lose?"

"Yep, shore did," Clyde returned. "He was bettin' pretty heavy and he lost a pile, but he could afford it. His daddy has a lot of money. Tom lost maybe three hundred dollars. Does that matter?"

"I don't know," Rufus answered, "but I'm thinkin' I'll ask him, first chance I get. Who else lost big?"

Well, lemme see," Preston mused. "Sam Mayberry lost a bundle, and Ben Johnson must'a lost a hundred. Ever'body lost but Sid."

"How 'bout the others?"

"Reckon they all lost more'n they could afford, but I'd say the Hannessey boy was the biggest loser. He plays a loose game."

A light rain was falling as Rufus left Clyde Preston's house. He was so lost in thought he didn't notice the glisten of raindrops on new leaves in Preston's front yard, or the dogwood bushes beginning to bud. He was thinking so hard that the next thing he knew he had crossed the river and was back on the road to Sylva.

Coming to Sue Hollifield's house on the edge of town, Rufus reined off the road and rode into her front yard. He left Fred with reins dangling and knocked on the front door. In a moment, he heard the patter of feet, and Sue opened the door.

"Why, Rufus!" she exclaimed. "Look at you! I never saw you so dressed up."

"No," Rufus said. "I don't think I have, either."

"Well, come on in. I'll put on some coffee."

He entered and sat before the fire, which quickly washed the chill of the morning from his bones.

Sue returned with two cups of coffee.

"What do I owe this visit to?" she asked. "I haven't seen so much of you lately."

"No, I ain't had no time. Been too busy tryin' to find a clue to Sid's killin'. But I think I've got one now."

"What?" she sat straighter in her chair, listening carefully.

"Did you know Sid won six hundred dollars in a poker game at Clyde Preston's house the night before he was killed?"

"Six hundred dollars!" she exclaimed. "No, I didn't. He didn't bring it home. He didn't even come home. Before he left, he told me he was going to the game and he probably wouldn't be back that night. He said he had to work the graveyard shift and would go straight from work to the campsite on Buff Creek. That's the last time I saw him."

"And he didn't give you the money?"

"No, he didn't. This is the first I've heard of it."

"Then he had six hundred dollars on him when he went into the woods."

"I suppose so. I don't know anything else he would have done with it."

"Well," Rufus said, "He didn't have it on him when we found him. We know he worked that night and left soon as he got off, goin' up to join the others. I'm a little surprised he didn't come by an' give you the money, though."

"Nothing strange about that," Sue said. "He often went up in the mountains without coming home after he worked graveyard."

"I'm gonna dig into this purty deep," Rufus said. "They's

only 'bout a dozen men who knew he won that money, unless he told somebody at work, but I think Sid was too careful to do that. Course, them who played spread the word around good, I guess."

"Have you talked with everybody who was in the game?"

"No, I ain't. I just heard of it 'bout a hour ago. But I will talk to 'em," he added, "an' I know who I'm gonna start with."

She knew better than to ask who.

He stood to leave and she said, "Rufus, you're right handsome, all dressed up like that."

"I feel like a clown," he said.

"No, don't. That outfit becomes you. You ought to forget about wearing overalls."

"That's crossed my mind," he answered, "especially when I walk down the street. This belt don't hurt at all no more. But I'll still wear my overhauls when I'm workin' on the farm."

That afternoon Rufus went up on his pasture hill, picked out a huge poplar tree and practiced shooting with his forty-five. He needed a while to get accustomed to the weight of the pistol and the way it bucked in his hand when he pulled the trigger.

But after an hour of practice, during which he shot up most of his ammunition, he was placing six shots from the six-shooter in the trunk of the tree.

He knocked off for the day with the intention of practicing at least once a week until he had shooting with the pistol to the point he wanted it.

Lissa Silver

FOURTEEN

Next morning, Rufus reported to Sheriff Clure about the poker game. Just as he finished, Sol Shulman knocked on and opened the door of the sheriff's office. "May I speak with you, Rufus?"

"Come on in," Clure said. "I'll leave you gentlemen alone for a while."

"No, no, Sheriff," Shulman said. "I just thought of three other men with big feet."

"Oh," Rufus questioned, "who?"

"Tom Hannessey is pretty near a thirteen," Shulman said. "Big feet. He's wearing a twelve and a half right now, but he's going to have to go to a thirteen before long. He's still growing."

"Is that so?" Rufus asked. "Tom Hannessey, huh?"

"Yes, sir, big feet; big, big feet. The other two are Clyde Preston, he's a twelve and a half, and Samson Reed from Balsam is an eleven and a half or twelve."

"Thanks, I've done eliminated some of them others," Rufus said. "We can eliminate Preston, too, but not Hannessey. I don't know Reed."

"We appreciate your telling us, Mister Shulman," the sheriff said. "If you think of any more, let us know."

"Oh, I shall," Shulman said, "I always like to be a help to the law. So long, gentlemen."

Rufus watched him walk across the street, turned to Clure, and said,

"Well, well! Danged if that don't beat all! Tom Hannessey! I'm gonna check into that right away, Sheriff. I have to say that I've suspected him all along and you know somethin', I never paid attention to the size of a man's feet. Guess it's good to notice everything about a man."

"Rufus," the sheriff appeared concerned, "don't let your heart get in the way of your head. The Hannessey boys, all of 'em, are bad business, so be careful. Don't get into something you can't get out of. There's three of them, you know, and they're boiling mad at you right now because you laid such a whupping on Charlie and Pete. So, go easy. Don't get backed in a corner, and don't be too hard on him till you've got hold of something definite. A man isn't guilty till he's proved so. There's a possibility you could be wrong, you know. I haven't seen anything to prove their guilt. It could'a been somebody else."

"Maybe so," Rufus answered. "But I think I'm right. I can feel it in my bones. I been thinkin' 'bout Tom Hannessey, an' I think I'm right. An' I ain't gonna get backed in no corner."

"It's your funeral. Go to it."

The Hannessey boys lived with their parents on top of Kings Mountain, just south of Sylva. Their father, Dabney, owned the Hole in the Wall Café in Sylva, a small, narrow eating place on Main Street. The road up the mountain was twisting and certainly tough for those new-fangled velocipedes like the Model T, Rufus thought, but it was a piece of cake for Fred, Rufus's sturdy mule.

On the way up, Rufus marveled at the view of the town. He had seen it from afar in the mountains before through field glasses, but it never looked like this—streets straight as arrows, well-painted businesses, grass greening along Scotts Creek on the far side of Back Street. Rufus and others had always called it Back Street but its official name was Mill Street.

Trees on Kings Mountain's highest elevations were budding. "Shore is beautiful from up here," Rufus said to Fred. "Don't know why anybody who lives in a place as purty as this'd want to be so ornery. But you just can't figure some people, Fred. Well, we'll see how the wind blows and try to get out of here in one piece. If I need your help, I'll whistle." He chuckled at the thought of Fred kicking down the doors to get in.

They rounded the last turn and before them stood the house, a large, two-story frame house painted white, a mansion for the time and place. The lawn was manicured and Mrs. Hannessey had planted tulips, which were blooming on both sides of the graveled walkway.

"Nice place," Rufus mused. "Hope they're home."

He ground-hitched Fred on the road near the house, went up the walkway, onto the porch, and knocked.

Mrs. Hannessey answered the door. "Oh, it's you, Rufus Raby. What do you want? You ain't welcome here after what you done to Charlie and Pete the other day."

"Ma'am," Rufus said, showing his badge. "This ain't no

social call. I'm here on official business, but I ain't forgot what yore boys done to my brother. Is Tom around?"

"He's here," she stepped back and beckoned Rufus to come in, ignoring his remark.

"Ma'am, I ain't no trouble-maker," Rufus said. "I'm on the other side. I try to stop trouble when it starts, an' I try to help people avoid it. Yore boys I whupped was tellin' lies on me an' Sue Hollifield an' laughing about it. I want to ask Tom some questions 'bout somethin' else, an' you're welcome to set in, if you want to."

"I don't want to," she snapped. "He's in there by the fire. Go on in." She nodded toward the spacious living room.

"It's kinda cold today, ain't it?" Rufus said. "A fire'll feel right good."

She did not respond but Tom Hannessey rose to his feet when Rufus entered, and the first thing Rufus did was stare at his huge feet.

"What the hell are you doing here?" Hannessey asked. "Ain't you got enough out of this family, the way you beat up Charlie and Pete?"

"Wasn't anything like that," Rufus said. "They was makin' bad remarks about me an' Sue Hollifield. I give 'em a little bit of what they deserved an' reminded them there was a whole lot more where that come from. And, like I told your mother, I ain't forgettin' what you done to my brother. Weren't no reason to kill him."

"We had to take Charlie to the doctor," Tom Hannessey said. He, too, ignored Rufus's remark. "You beat him so bad it knocked his back plumb out of joint."

"His fault," Rufus said. "He fell over the counter. If he'd kept his big mouth shut, I wouldn't a'touched him. And don't forget we had to have the doctor an' the undertaker with my brother. You don't have no complaint with me."

"Well, you're here. What do you want?"

"Wanna talk a little business with you."

"Go ahead, but make it short."

"Don't know as I can do that," Rufus said. "You may be in a little trouble. Maybe a whole lot."

"'Bout what?" Tom asked, frowning.

"Gimme straight answers and this may not take so long," Rufus said.

"Shoot."

"Where was you an' Charlie an' Pete the night Sid Hollifield was killed?"

"You ain't tryin' to pin that on us, are you?"

"Well, I dunno. You got pretty big feet, I notice. What size shoe do you wear?"

"What difference does it make how big my shoes are? Ain't none of your business," Tom replied, and Rufus could tell that he was self-conscious about the size of his feet. "What you want to know that for, anyway?"

"Well, the only tracks we found around their campsite the next day was them of somebody who had big feet, like maybe twelve an' a half or thirteen."

"Weren't mine," Tom answered.

"Look," said Rufus, "I know we ain't the best of friends, but I need some information from you an' I'm gonna stay here till I get it. Answer my question. Where was you?"

"You know where I was. I was playing poker in the same game Sid Hollifield was in," Tom replied.

"What time did you leave?" Rufus asked. "How long after Sid left did you stay?"

"I don't know," Tom said. "I didn't look at no clock. Somewhere around midnight, I guess. Long enough to try to get some of my money back."

"How much money did you lose to Sid?"

"That ain't none of your business!"

"Maybe it ain't an' maybe it is," Rufus said. "You could'a wanted to get your money back from him. I know you lost a hundred or two. You could'a left in plenty of time to be in the woods that mornin' when Sid was comin' down. Did Sid say anything about goin' coon huntin'?"

"I dunno. I didn't hear him if he did."

The door through which Rufus had entered the room opened, and Charlie and Pete Hannessey came in. Their lips were puffed and bandaged in places and their eyes registered surprise when they saw Rufus. One of Pete's eyes was swollen half shut and black.

"What are you doin' here?" Charlie asked.

"I come to see Tom," Rufus said, "but maybe all three of you ought'a come down town with me. Got some questions for you."

"I answered mine," Tom said. "If you don't believe me, go and ask anybody who was in the game."

"I plan to do exactly that," Rufus said.

Slowly, the other two boys edged toward Rufus, separating to come up on both sides.

Rufus paid them no noticeable attention, but said to Tom, "If you don't want things made hard for you, you better call off your dogs. Tell 'em I done talked to them once this week. If they want me to talk to 'em again, why go ahead, but a lot of nice things in here'll get busted, includin' your heads.

"You could be in some trouble, Tom. Them, too. You better call 'em off. I ain't kiddin'."

"Boys," Tom said to his brothers, "this ain't no fightin' affair. It's sheriff's business, so set down and let him alone."

Rufus squared around. "If you don't do as he says, we'll just have at it right here. I ain't a'scared of all three of you, an' remember, the law's on my side."

"We don't care nothin' about no law," Pete said. "We're gonna work you over, Rufus."

"Not before I ask you the same question I just asked your brother," Rufus pulled the forty-five from his holster, cocked it, and held it beside his leg, pointing at the floor. "Now, shut up, and set down. This here thing's loaded."

Startled at the sight of the big forty-five, they pulled up chairs and sat. Rufus slipped his pistol off cock but held it in his lap, and looked at both of them. "Boys," he said, "we had some trouble over at Velt's because you two big mouths said some bad things that ain't true about Sue Hollifield an' me. We'll let that ride for now. I won't forget it, but I better not hear you're doin' it ag'in. Now, tell me where you two was at the night Sid Hollifield was killed, an' be quick about it."

"Wouldn't you like to know?" Charlie said in a surly voice.

Rufus kicked the chair from beneath himself and stood up, brandishing the shooting iron. He thought he was being dramatic, but it worked.

"You better speak an' be quick about it," he said. "I'm 'bout to take the three of you downtown right now."

"We was shootin' pool," Charlie capitulated, calming down and eying Rufus's huge pistol.

"Where?"

"Over at the pool hall," said Pete. "We was there till about two o'clock in the mornin' an' then we come home."

"You better be tellin' the truth," Rufus said, returning his forty-five to its holster, "cause I'm gonna stop there an' ask Mr. Phillips if you was there that night."

"Go ahead an' ask him," Charlie said. "We ain't lyin'. Got no cause to. We didn't have nothin' to do with Sid's death."

Rufus turned toward the door. "All right. I hope you're tellin' me the truth, but if you ain't, you're in big trouble. You too, Tom."

At that moment, the door opened again and Mrs. Hannessey came in with a broom in her hand. "Rufus Raby," she said scornfully, "you get out'a here right now and hit the trail back downtown."

"Sorry, Mrs. Hannessey," Rufus replied, "but I have business here. Sheriff's business. If you'd like to join us, you're free to do so. I just asked your boys where they was the night Sid Hollifield was murdered, an' I'm askin' you the same question. I wanna see if they're lyin'."

"Lyin'?" she asked. "My boys lyin'? My boys don't lie. You must be outta your mind."

"We'll see," said Rufus. "We'll see."

"They were right here at home," Mrs. Hannessey said.

"Their story's a little different than yours," Rufus said. "They said they shot pool downtown till two in the mornin'."

"Well, they'd know better than I would remember," she said. "My memory ain't what it used to be."

"What time did they come home?"

"I don't know what time it was, but they was here when I got up."

"What time was that?"

"I always get up by ten, or maybe eleven or twelve. I haven't felt well lately."

Rufus looked from one boy to the other, and then to the third. "You boys hang around home for a while. I may be comin' back to take you downtown an' let Sheriff Clure talk to you. He'll probably ask the same questions I did—an' some more. You're suspects in a murder case."

Their mouths fell open, but they said no more.

Rufus turned on his heel, and walked out.

Returning to the sheriff's office, Rufus stopped at the pool hall, and asked Fred Phillips what time the boys left the night Sid was killed.

"They left at midnight," Phillips said.

"Midnight!" Rufus exclaimed. "They said it was two o'clock in the morning."

"Wasn't that late," Phillips said. "I close up at midnight."

"I'm thankin' you," Rufus said. He climbed on Fred and rode on to the sheriff's office.

Lissa Silver©

FIFTEEN

Rufus was grinning when he entered the office.

Clure looked up from his desk, peered behind Rufus, and said, "Don't see no prisoners, Rufe. Have some bad luck?"

"No, sir," Rufus returned. "No bad luck a'tall."

"What'd you find out then?"

"I dunno," Rufus admitted, "but I had a talk with 'em and I think they're lyin' an' guilty as sin."

"What makes you think so."

"Well, I talked to all three boys," Rufus began, "an' to their mother, too. Being perfectly honest with you, John, any or all of them boys could'a made it into the woods 'fore daylight. They had plenty of time to ambush Sid comin' down the mountain and carry his body up to where I found him, or they might'a found him in camp. The other hunters didn't get back to camp till about six o'clock."

"Why do you say that?"

"They get mixed up tryin' to get their stories straight. An' their mother took up for 'em, but she couldn't get anything straight, either. Got about two different answers for ever' question I asked her."

"Tell me how they could have gotten him into a cave full of rattlesnakes?"

"Been thinkin' 'bout that," Rufus said. "I guess rattlesnakes got to sleep, just like we do, don't they?

"Reckon they do," said the sheriff. "Don't tell me they tippy-toed up."

"No, I don't think nothin' like that," Rufus replied. "I figger they shoved him in the cave on a long plank."

"How's that?"

"On a long plank."

"Say they did," the sheriff mused, seriously, "Somebody would have to get close enough to stir up the snakes, and how'd they get him off the plank?"

"That's easy," Rufus replied. "Just turned the plank over and throwed him off. He was layin' sort'a on his side when I found him."

"But how did they get the plank up there that close to the snakes?" "Somebody could have wore real tall boots, like wadin' boots, stuffed with cotton or rags to keep fangs that came through from reaching him. A snake can't strike higher than half the length of its body, so a man fixed up like that would be fairly safe from snakebite.

"They's three of 'em. Two could'a carried Sid—they're big, strong boys—and the other carried the plank."

The sheriff thought for a moment, rubbing his chin, with a serious look on his face. "Reckon it'd be possible," he said, "but don't go too fast on this. We'd need more than supposition."

"What the heck is that?" Rufus asked.

"It means you ain't got no positive proof. You're just supposing. All you got is what you're thinking, Rufus, but keep on it. You could be right, and," he added, "you could be wrong."

Rufus studied the floor a minute, then said, "I know it's just my thinkin', Sheriff, but I been givin' it a lot of thought. I know they ain't gonna be guilty till we prove 'em so, an' I'm hearin' you when you tell me I may not be thinking' straight, but they're the only suspects I can think of right now. They may be some others come along; I'll be keepin' my eyes open for 'em. I ain't convicted them boys, yet, but Charlie an' Pete said they shot pool till two in the mornin' an' Mr. Phillips said he closed at midnight an' they left then.

"All right," said the sheriff, "you did get something to go on."

Rufus said. "I've got a gut feelin' and my head tells me they're the ones who done it."

"We need more than that," the sheriff said. "That's still supposition. But we know he was killed by the blow to the head, probably by a rifle stock. And we've got a thirty-caliber bullet. How many people do you know around here who has a .30-30?"

"I've got one," Rufus said, "but we know I didn't kill him. Let's see now. Bob and Bill Shuler, Clyde Rector, and Burl and Ralph Henson have got .30-30s."

"Who else?"

"Sid Frady's got one," Rufus replied. "I know Clyde Preston and Clayton Evans have .30-30s, then there's Ben Johnson—and Skeeter Smith over on Savannah. Tom Jones has one at Addie, and Lewis Blanton's got one. He bear hunts some. Sid had one; I guess it's over at his house. An', let's see, who else? Sam Cope has one."

Sheriff Clure spoke up, "Well, I want every .30-30 in

the county test fired. Spread the word to all who have them and ask them to bring them to the sheriff's office. You don't have to tell 'em why."

SIXTEEN

On his way to work the next morning, Rufus, carrying his own .30-30, stopped by Sue's house. When she answered his knock, she opened the door wide and said, "Come in, Rufus. I'll fix you some breakfast."

"Thank you, Sue," he said. "I ate breakfast about five this mornin'."

"Then you'd better come in," she said. "That was five hours ago. You must be hungry by now."

"No, I ain't," he said. "I just stopped by to pick up Sid's rifle, his .30-30. Sheriff wants to test-fire all the .30-30s in the county."

"Why?" she asked.

"Well, I didn't tell you." he said. "Didn't think it meant no difference but it does now. Sid was shot after he was already dead. Sheriff thinks if we can find the gun that shot him, we can find his killers."

"I'll get it," she said, and in a moment she returned with Sid's .30-30 Winchester.

"Thanks, Sue," Rufus said, "I'll take you up on breakfast one o' these days."

When Rufus came in to the sheriff's office, he carried three .30-30s. "Here's the Hannessey rifle," he said. "They didn't much want me to have it, but I insisted a little, an' they saw the light."

“I’m not going to ask how much light they saw,” Sheriff Clure said, and Rufus grinned.

“That might be a good idea,” he said. “These other two are mine an’ Sid’s.”

“Now we have to find a way to fire them without ruining the bullets,” the sheriff said.

“We can get a big wooden box an’ fill it with dry sand or dirt,” Rufus said. “That’ll hold bullets an’ won’t mark ’em any.”

“Okay, you get a box and bring it here,” Sheriff Clure said. “We’ll test the rifles behind the building. Might spread the word up and down the street that if they hear firing they shouldn’t pay any attention to it.”

“I’ll do that,” Rufus said, and left.

In the basement of the hardware, Rufus sawed the boards and nailed together a wooden box large enough, when filled with sand or dirt, to stop the bullets. Then he walked up Back Street, carrying the box, and stopped where workmen were mixing concrete to make a portion of a new basement floor beneath Velt’s Café.

“Howdy, Luke,” he said to the job foreman. “We need some sand. Gonna test-fire a lot of rifles over behind the jail. Need dry sand, maybe about a bushel.”

Luke Wilson said, “Well, there’s a whole pile of it outside. Help yourself.”

Rufus filled the box with sand and asked Luke to help him carry it up the steps to Velt’s Cafe and across the street to the sheriff’s office, and the foreman obliged. They placed it in the narrow alley behind the office, and Rufus reported to the sheriff that they could start any time.

"Let's wait till we get more rifles. Only got four right now."

"Four?" Rufus questioned. "Whose is the fourth one?"

"Mine," said the sheriff.

Lissy Silver©

SEVENTEEN

It was plowing time when Rufus hitched his horse Bill to a plow and began a long furrow in his corn field. He thought of Sue and realized he was spending a lot of time thinking about her, especially when he was alone working on the farm. Until today, Rufus hadn't realized how different he felt lately; he had just enjoyed it. He had never been in love, didn't even know what love was, but he knew he felt something special within when he thought of Sue. She was beautiful. And nice. And very intelligent. What buffaloed Rufus was the thought of Sue falling in love with a rascal like himself. Though he couldn't swear that she had, he just didn't think it possible.

He had no qualities to match hers. He didn't know what qualities were, but he had heard someone say it in the context of comparing a person with another—and he thought it was a good word. He would try to remember it and say it sometime to Sue.

Confound it! There he went again!

He stopped Bill, scotched the plow on its side, and sat down in the clods to try and think about his feelings.

In the house, his mother looked out the window and saw him sitting in the furrow. A woeful look of compassion came over her face, and she looked upward at the ceiling and quietly said, "Lord, he'p him."

She knew he was all torn up over Sue, figured that he was in love with her but didn't know it himself. She thought it was the best thing that could ever happen to him, providing Sue fell in love with him.

"He needs her bad, Lord," she uttered, and went back to work cleaning the house.

With the spring sun warm on his back, Rufus pondered. He knew he had his good points, but he also admitted to himself that he had too many bad ones. One was how much time he spent on Possum Branch making whiskey. Another was drinking it. If he didn't make and sell a batch now and then, Rufus wasn't sure he made enough money otherwise to keep up the farm and make ends meet. On moonshine sales, he made a dollar a pint, two dollars a quart, and six dollars a gallon, plus fifty cents for the jug. Shucks, a gallon was worth almost as much as a week of his wages!

It seemed that Sue was on his mind all the time. It was early spring and he spent a lot of time alone plowing his fields, preparing them for spring planting. He also had so many other chores to do to keep the farm working that he hardly had time to spend in town working with the sheriff. The eight dollars he was paid by the county every week certainly wasn't enough. While Rufus worked the farm, he was on call by the sheriff, but the town was quiet these days and Rufus got his plowing in.

"I ain't got a lick o' sense," he told himself, sitting there in the field. "Got no business thinkin' 'bout Sue so much. I ain't in her class, an' I know I don't stand no chance with her. Somebody else'll come along an' get her. I ain't got no business fallin' in love—if that's what I'm doin'. I know it, Ma knows it, I suspect Fred knows it, an' maybe Bill, too. Shucks, could be the whole town knows it." He didn't realize how close that thought came to the truth.

"Might be even Sue knows it; she's been awful nice to me lately." That thought stopped him. "Why? Why was she being so nice to him. Was it because of his friendship with Sid—and with her, too, of course? Or was it because he had found Sid's body and had been the one who came to tell her of his killing? Or, it could be because she liked him personally and had nobody else to lean on during these lonely, trying days."

He couldn't answer one of those questions, couldn't even guess.

So he turned his thoughts back to Bill and the plow, and in moments he was again plowing straight furrows in the ground—and thinking about Sue.

It occurred to him that he should spend more time with her to keep her from missing Sid so much and being so lonesome, and he savored the idea. After all, he hadn't seen much of her through the winter.

Lissa Silver®

EIGHTEEN

Rufus left the house the next morning, bound for the sheriff's office in Sylva. He was in the barn, bridling Fred when he heard someone call, "Rufus? Are you in there, Rufus?" His face began to redden; it was Sue calling him.

He stepped outside and she sat her horse in the yard. She was peering toward the barn.

"There you are," she said, laughing. It seemed to Rufus that she was always happy. "I thought I saw you go in."

She looked so lovely he could hardly stand it, figuring an ignoramus like himself stood no chance with her.

"Gettin' ready to go to work," Rufus said. "Got some things to do today."

"I won't keep you but a minute," she said. "I'm going up the creek to check on Mrs. Cogdill. I heard she has been sick."

"She has," he said. "Ma went up to see her last night and said she ain't doin' too good."

"I heard that, too," Sue said. She paused a moment, then asked, "Rufus, will you take me to church Sunday morning?"

That stopped him in his tracks.

"Church?" he said.

"You don't have to if you don't want to."

"Well, I reckon I do want to. Shore I will."

"Good. Can you pick me up about ten-thirty?"

"Shore can. I'll bring th' buggy."

"Good," she said. "I love to ride a buggy."

"Me, too," he said. "It's shore a smooth ride."

"I think Reverend Snyder will be happy to see you, Rufus."

"Might be," he answered. "I ain't seen him in a coupl'a months—'cept at Sid's funeral, an' he didn't see me then."

"That's why I want you to go," she said, looking serious. "You need to go to church, Rufus."

"How come?"

"Everybody ought to go to church."

"Reckon so," he answered. "I ain't been in a long time. The preacher probably don't even remember what I look like."

"I know. Reverend Snyder asked me to bring you, but that isn't why I'm asking. I want you to take me. A good man ought to be in church, and I would be honored to have you take me."

"Gosh!" he exclaimed. "Reckon I ain't such a good man."

"Reverend Snyder thinks you are."

"Well, I'll be blowed! Didn't know he even knowed me."

"Everybody knows you, Rufus, and everybody likes you. That's another reason you should go."

"Reckon ever'body don't know me, and some don't even like me."

"I haven't heard anyone say that."

"Then they're thinkin' it. I ain't so pop'lar with some people."

"I like you, Rufus," she said softly. "You're a good man, a tender man, and that's another reason why you should be in church. And I just said more than I can say for most men around here."

That stopped him. His mouth fell open. He wanted to ask how much she liked him, but his knees turned to water. He gulped and swallowed hard and blurted, "I better get on to town. I'll see you Sunday mornin'."

"Ten-thirty," she said. "Remember, now."

"I ain't likely to ferget," he said as he turned and boarded Fred.

Lissa Silver©

NINETEEN

Elated over this turn of events with Sue, Rufus sang his heart out riding to town. He didn't care who heard him, so happy was he. The road was deserted of other people, however, but he saw an occasional horse or cow raise its head and stare at him and once he saw the white flash of a deer's tail as it bolted through the woods away from him.

You ought to see my Cindy,
She lives away down south.
She's so sweet the honey bees
Swarm around her mouth.

She loved me on the mountainside,
She loved me on the hill,
And ever' time she said "I won't"
Her echo said "I will."

Get along home, Cindy, Cindy,
Get along home, Cindy, Cindy,
Get along home, Cindy, Cindy,
I'll marry you some day.

Rufus reported to Sheriff Clure that morning and was amazed at the number of .30-30 rifles stacked in the corner, each one tagged with the owner's name.

"I see we're ready for business," Rufus said. "How many we got?"

"I haven't counted them yet," the sheriff answered. "I guess maybe twenty-five or thirty."

"How'd you get 'em?"

"I just put out word, and fellers brought them in. I asked each one if they knew anybody else with one, and I picked up three or four more thataway."

"Guess I better get busy then," Rufus said and gathered up an armload of rifles.

When the shooting started, merchants nearby reached under their counters and brought out their own weapons, thirty-eight revolvers, two or three forty-fives, and assorted others, fearing something was happening.

They peered out the front windows of their stores but saw nothing out of line. Stepping out on the street, they heard rifle shots coming from behind the sheriff's office, and realized that the test-firing of the county's .30-30s had begun.

Rufus fired the first one into the box of sand. Putting the rifle aside, he dug out the bullet, saw that it was not scarred, and dropped it in a small bag, which he attached to the trigger guard. Each rifle also had a tag with its owner's name on it.

Then he reached for another rifle.

The shooting took up most of the morning. It was not fast work, and the heavy boom of the rifles reverberated up and down Main Street. Rufus had to dig out each slug, brush sand off it, bag it, and attach it to the rifle. By noontime he had test-fired thirty rifles.

More were coming in, but Rufus put off firing them until another day. The sheriff had set up a microscope on a table in the office, and as soon as Rufus finished the first day's firing, they took shifts examining the bullets under the microscope.

The sheriff showed Rufus how to scope the bullets and what to look for, and he caught on quickly, even though he had never seen a microscope before.

After the thirty had been scanned, a match had not been found.

"Ain't likely to find one," said the sheriff. "Whoever shot Sid probably hid his gun and unless we can find out who-all didn't bring their rifles in, this may not even work."

On the following morning, Rufus finished his shooting duty and still no match was found. He had checked forty-three rifles. There were a lot more in the county, he knew, because Jackson County was deer and bear-hunting country in season, and that required heavy rifles.

That afternoon, owners of the rifles began coming in from all over the county to claim their weapons. Clure asked each again if he knew of someone who might not have turned his rifle in and checked off each man mentioned on a list he had made of rifles tested.

When the rifle-owners had been cleared out of the office, Sheriff Clure said to Rufus: "Maybe we're going about this wrong. Could be we need to narrow our field. We ought to coordinate this search from Sylva up the Asheville Road to Balsam and concentrate on testing all the rifles in that area first, because that's where all the participants of the hunt came from. Then if we don't find anything there, we'll pick another quadrant of the county and search it. We're trying to cover too big a field to take the county as a whole at the same time.

"It's likely, I think, that the rifle that shot Sid came from our sector from here to Balsam, so let's concentrate our efforts in that area."

"How do you want to go about it?" Rufus asked.

"I think you ought to take a couple of days, ride up that way and knock on every door you come to and ask if the man of the house has a .30-30 rifle. Like we're doing, we're not contacting all the rifle owners in any one sector."

"When you want me to start?"

"Today I guess. You ought to be able to visit every house from here to Addie today. Being farming country, there ain't more houses in that whole area that you can't contact today."

The sheriff thought a moment, then said, "Can you drive a car?"

"Reckon I can," Rufus answered, "Ain't much to it."

"I'll check with the county commissioners," Clure said. "We have enough left in our budget for the year to buy a car, and we really ought to have one ourselves. We can't police this whole county a'horseback. I'll go see the commissioner right now."

An hour later, the sheriff returned. Rufus was snoozing, with his feet up on the sheriff's desk. "Wake up, Rufus; let's go get us a car. Mayor says it'll be all right, seeing as how we need one so bad for this job."

An hour later, a new Model T Ford stood before the sheriff's office, filled with oil and gas and an extra can of gasoline in the rear.

"You can start any time, Rufus," Clure said. "She's ready to go."

Rufus's thoughts were running in a different direction at the time. Deep within himself, he resented having to bring each gun to the sheriff to tag. The only thing he could do was tie the tag to the trigger guard. He couldn't fill them out. He told himself that his ma was right when she told him he ought to learn to read and write. He had never given it much thought until the business of tagging the rifles came up, and he determined to do something about it—however, he knew he could never bring himself to sit with a room full of first graders and learn to read and write at the schoolhouse. Besides, he thought, he could never fit in one of them first-grade chairs with his knees up around his ears.

Sunday morning came and the church bell rang as Rufus and Sue pulled into the church yard in his buggy, which he had equipped with extra cushions for a more comfortable ride. The church had no Sunday school rooms, only the sanctuary.

Rufus was dressed in his Sunday finest—clean, pressed trousers, a shirt open at the neck, and one of his pa's suit coats, which was a size too small for his hefty frame, but he felt dressed up wearing it.

Sue looked like a million dollars, he thought, dressed in

a long blue skirt and a frilly white blouse, for the weather was quite warm that day. Her beautiful dark hair flowed down her back.

"I love it," Sue said as Rufus parked the buggy in front of the church. "I love to ride the buggy and I love taking you to church, Rufus, because Reverend Snyder seemed to want you to come so badly."

"How 'bout you?" Rufus asked.

"I did too," she said, rather demurely

Rufus stepped down from the buggy and walked around and helped Sue to the ground. They walked into church side by side and drew stares from the folks who were already in the building. Sue saw a couple of women whisper to other women, all of whom sat in the pews on the right. She took a seat in an empty pew on that side of the church, and Rufus found a seat in the men's side to the left.

A woman turned and stared at Sue, who smiled sweetly back and directed her attention to the pulpit where Clyde Preston, the Sunday School superintendent, was making announcements. When Preston finished, he walked back to the pew on which Rufus sat, winked at him, and sat beside him.

The congregation broke into small groups, largely according to sex and age, and gathered by class in the corners of the room. One class met in the choir area, and Sunday school began. Children's classes met in the church yard. The spring weather allowed that today.

"I see you and Sue are getting' pretty thick," Preston whispered to Rufus, but Rufus only stared back for a moment, and said nothing.

When Sunday school ended, both men and women returned to their original seats and the Reverend Snyder walked into the pulpit. He looked at those sitting on each side of the church and finally began to talk.

"I am pleased with the turnout on this beautiful spring morning," he said, "and happy to see that we have a visitor in our fine deputy sheriff, Rufus Raby."

He nodded to Rufus and people turned to stare at Rufus, watching his face redden at the attention given him.

A portion of the sermon concerned those men, unnamed of course, who persisted in the manufacture of illegal corn whiskey, even though any other work that paid a living wage was hard to come by in Jackson County.

Rufus realized Reverend Snyder was stepping all over his toes, which he took personally. He was embarrassed with the thought that he had been singled out by the preacher. He felt it deeply, and even though the thought was in his mind only, he felt a bit testy, because there were a half-dozen other men seated in the church who made moonshine on the side. For some, he thought, it was their only income. Without it, babies might starve.

The sermon was pure fire and brimstone of the hottest nature, and Rufus was sure it was directed almost entirely at him. He had no idea why, especially with men sitting around him who made whiskey, too.

Some of the sermon concerned the ladies who tried to outdress each other, which the reverend called an unwise expenditure of their husbands' hard-earned money, and a sin against the Holy Ghost, but Rufus didn't understand all of that, especially the big words. He caught only a word of that portion of the sermon here and there. He had no idea who the Holy Ghost was.

Oddly, he also felt relief flood his being when Reverend Snyder changed the subject to the sin of playing cards that he said takes bread off the family tables—or someone else's—which the Lord didn't favor any more than the killing of Sid Hollifield.

Why did the preacher have to drag up Sid's murder? Rufus wondered. He looked over at Sue and she was daubing at her eyes with a handkerchief. Rufus felt like walking out but didn't for Sue's sake.

In a few minutes he hushed and sat down.

When church turned out, the congregation waited until Reverend Snyder walked down the aisle after he finished his closing prayer, and out the door and stopped at the foot of the church steps to greet the people on their way out.

Sue joined Rufus before they reached the door and they walked out together.

"Good morning, Sue," said the preacher, who then turned to Rufus and said, "Mr. Raby, I am pleased that you saw fit to join us this morning. It is good to see an officer of the law sitting in a pew on Sabbath morning. I hope it will not be the last time you come."

"I'll think about it," Rufus answered curtly.

"I believe Sue will see to that. Am I right, Sue?"

She nodded and said, "I hope so, Reverend," and knowing that the whiskey-making part of the sermon had been directed at Rufus, and realizing how he resented it, she wondered if she would ever be able to get him back to church.

On the way home, Sue asked Rufus if he would stay for lunch, and he nodded in the affirmative. "I guess I might as well," he said and then exaggerated, "Ever'body in the county saw me in church this mornin' an' heard what the preacher had to say, or at least they'll know it by supper time."

"They were pleased to see you, Rufus, and I doubt that anyone would say anything wrong about your coming to my house for lunch after church, and even if they did, we'll just ignore it."

He nodded in agreement, and she asked, "Were you comfortable? Did going to church hurt as much as you thought it would?"

Both laughed at Sue's little joke, and Rufus answered, "Didn't hurt much 'cept that part about making a little corn squeezings now and then. Half the men in the church make liquor, but he said all of that straight to me. That's how some of us make a livin'. I might try to go again some time."

"Will you come next Sunday?" Sue asked, and it occurred to her that she was the only reason Rufus had agreed to come in the first place. That thought created a warmth inside of her. However, she felt that the efforts on her part were worth the result because Rufus was beginning to dig his thoughts into the darker part of his life.

"Yeah, if you'll let me take you with me."

"All right," she said, "it's a date," and Rufus looked at her and began to smile.

"Didn't hurt as much as I thought it might," Rufus said, "but I didn't see the sheriff there."

"He doesn't come often," she said. "Just sometimes."

Next morning, when Rufus walked into the sheriff's office, Clure smiled at him. "Hear you joined the congregation yesterday."

"Didn't join nothin'," Rufus said. "I just went to church."

"That's what I was told. Fact is, that was the big talk around town yesterday afternoon."

"What?" Rufus asked.

"You being in church. Heard a lot of people say they didn't think they'd seen you there before, but most seemed glad you came. Some said they hoped you wouldn't quit coming because of what the preacher said about you."

"Hadn't been before," Rufus said, "but might go again next Sunday."

"Yes," the sheriff said thoughtfully. "Don't blame you a bit. You and Sue make a nice couple. Folks liked to see the two of you come in together.

"The wife said you did just fine," Clure added, "and she said that people liked to see you there. Maybe you ought to make it a habit."

"Felt kinda like a twelve-toed boy at a swimmin' party, all them folks a'lookin' at me, but I'll probably be there next Sunday."

"I think that would be nice," Clure said, and changed the subject. "We'll get back to testing the rifles in the morning. Got a few more in yesterday, so if you'll come on in, you can shoot 'em into your little box."

"Do you really expect to find the killer thataway?" Rufus asked.

"Don't know," Clure answered. "Doubt it. Sometimes cases are solved by the smallest things. Doesn't hurt to try, does it?"

"No, don't hurt me," Rufus answered. "I like to shoot, only I never shot in no box before."

Rufus shot seventeen more rifles into the box the next day and checked all of them in the microscope, but found no matches.

"Don't know whether this is workin' or not," Rufus said. "what do you think?"

"I don't know, either," said the sheriff. "But it shows the town that we're working on the case, and who knows what it might stir up. Might be we'll find somebody who didn't bring his gun in, and then we'll have something to start with, anyway."

"That's sort'a what I been figgering," Rufus said, and the sheriff was pleased.

"I'm proud of you, Rufus. You're catching on to things quick. You're going to be a fine deputy. Might have to rub some of your rough edges down a little, but we can do that."

"Figger I need that," Rufus said, "but I like the job. Gives me somethin' to do that makes me feel good an' makes me think, so I'm ready to learn 'bout anything you want to teach me."

The sheriff beamed. He was pleased with the answer. "By the way," Clure said, "Commissioner Norton said he'd raised you to ten dollars a week 'cause you're working so hard for the county's sake."

"I want to find who killed Sid for Sid's sake" Rufus said, and in a moment added in a lower voice, "an' fer Sue's."

Thinking about what he had thought of Sue's loneliness, Rufus went to see her on Monday afternoon. She made sandwiches for their lunch and lemonade later, and they sat in the porch swing and talked the afternoon away.

When he left he thought his coming had made Sue feel better, at least he thought he had taken her mind off Sid's death for a while.

She kissed him lightly on the cheek when he left and this time he didn't fall down the steps. He was beginning to like it.

"Hmmm," he thought, riding Fred away, "maybe I'm makin' some headway."

Progress within himself, he thought; but it didn't occur to him that he might be making progress with Sue, also. On that point, he was quite afraid to think she was leaning in that direction. After all, they were just good friends.

"Ain't that it?" he asked himself aloud.

TWENTY

On the following Sunday morning, Sue and Rufus arrived at church a few minutes before the meeting began.

"Don't see why we can't sit together," Rufus said. "We come together an' ever'body knows it."

"That's the way churches are," Sue said. "They split the women to one side and men to the other. It's something Biblical, I think. Maybe it will change one of these days. I hope so."

They sat through another sermon in which the Reverend Snyder commented again on the Devil's brew while looking straight at Rufus, who tried to keep from squirming. He was on the verge of anger at the end of the service.

When they walked out together and the preacher shook their hands, he said, "Rufus, I hope you're absorbing my sermons."

"Don't know what that word means," Rufus answered, "but are you talkin' just to me or to all them other fellers who make a little run now and then?"

"Well, I'm hoping you don't forget what I'm preaching against," the preacher said.

"Oh, I ain't a'gonna forget it," Rufus said, and speaking loud enough for several people around them to hear, he added, "an' I ain't a'gonna forget that pint you got from me a while back!"

The preacher frowned, and Sue hurried Rufus on toward the buggy, and as Henry Smith walked by, he looked at Rufus and winked.

"He bought a pint from me, too," Henry said, and both he and Rufus laughed, breaking Rufus's tension.

As they left the church yard, Sue looked at Rufus and giggled. "Way to go, cowboy," she said.

"Hope you ain't mad at me," Rufus said seriously.

"Not in the least," she said. "I felt he was speaking to you unjustly this morning. Last week was enough, but today he deserved what you said to him. I don't think he'll make the same mistake next Sunday and I hope this won't make you stop going."

"Oh, I ain't a'gonna stop goin'. I'll take you to church as long as you want me to. I just don't want to get preached at ever' Sunday."

When they reached Sue's house, Rufus tied off the reins, descended the buggy and helped Sue down.

"You will have lunch with me, won't you?" she asked.

"Yes," Rufus replied. "I ain't mad at nobody, not even the preacher, but I hope he don't pick on me no more."

"I seriously doubt he will," Sue laughed.

During lunch, Rufus was quiet, as if he were thinking seriously of something.

Finally, Sue spoke up. "You're not still thinking about that sermon, are you?"

"No, I ain't," Rufus answered. "Got somethin' else on my mind I want to talk to you about, Sue."

She gave him a serious glance and asked, "What is it?"

"I want to learn to read an' write, and talk better," he blurted, "but I don't want to have to set in school with no first graders to do it."

"Why, Rufus, you don't have to go to school to learn that," she said with delight in her voice. "I'll teach you to read and write, and I'll help you speak better, if you wish, and count, too."

"Reckon I was hopin' you'd say that, Sue. I'll shore consider it a favor. I don't want to be ignorant the rest of my life."

"What brought this on?" Sue asked.

"Well, the other day when we was taggin' rifles after I shot 'em in the box, I was a little embarrassed that I couldn't fill out the tags myself. Sheriff had to write 'em out an' I put 'em on the guns."

"We will fix that," she said.

"How long you think it'll take?"

"You're a smart guy," she said. "It won't take as long as you think. We can start tomorrow evening, here at the house."

"Sounds good to me," he replied, and the two went on with lunch.

On Monday, after work, Rufus pecked on Sue's front door. She opened the door and said, "Hi, Rufus, come on in; we're all set up."

She led him into the parlor and in a corner sat a small blackboard.

They went to work immediately. First she wrote the ABCs on the board, both in capitals and in small letters.

"First thing we have to do," she said, "is learn the ABCs." She handed him a sheet of paper on which she had written them out, too.

They spent two hours going over the ABCs and at the end of the session Rufus could almost say them by heart.

"Take that sheet home with you," she said, "and practice them every spare moment you get."

At the door, Rufus turned to Sue and said, "Hope you won't tell nobody about this."

"Oh, I won't. One day soon you'll surprise everyone in town."

He bade her good night, climbed aboard Fred, and rode away.

The next evening when he showed up, he could say the ABCs through without missing a letter.

"That's good, Rufus, very good," Sue said. "Now, let's get you started on some words."

She printed in capitals the word CAT on the board.

"Read the letters," she said.

"Cee, uh, A, an' T," he stammered.

"Right. What does that spell? Figure it out."

After a couple of minutes, she said, "The first letter is what?"

"Cee," Rufus said.

"All right. You're not trying to say cee. Used this way it's K, K, K."

"K," Rufus said, "K, K."

"Put the A to it," Sue said. "Like in apple."

"K, a—k, a," Rufus sounded.

"Right," she said. "Now add the T."

"K,a,t. Cat!' Rufus exclaimed.

"Wonderful, now let's sound out some others," said Sue proudly.

She printed DOG, COW, BILL, and FRED on the board, and after a couple of hours Rufus was reading all of them.

His chest swelled with pride, and Sue was so happy she kissed him, whereupon he clasped his hands to her shoulders, drew her to him, and kissed her on the mouth. She responded, and in a moment, when they broke apart, she uttered, "Oh, Rufus. . . ."

"I'm sorry," he apologized. "Don't know what made me do that."

"Please don't apologize. I've wondered how long it would take you to get around to that."

He kissed her again, and before Rufus's heat swelled into a flame, she said, "It's time to end. I'll see you tomorrow evening."

When Rufus mounted Fred, he burst into song and Sue stood in the doorway listening until he rode out of earshot.

She'll be comin' round the mountain when she
comes—when she comes,
She'll be comin' round the mountain when she
comes—when she comes,
She'll be comin' round the mountain,
She'll be comin' round the mountain,
She'll be comin' round the mountain, when she
comes—when she comes.

His voice clearly reached her ears as he sang the second verse.

She'll be ridin' in a wagon when she comes—
when she comes,
She'll be ridin' in a wagon when she comes—
when she comes,
She'll be ridin' in a wagon,
And her feet'll be a'draggin',
She'll be ridin' in a wagon when she comes—
when she comes.

Sue laughed herself to sleep that night.

Next morning, Nettie Jones stopped by the sheriff's office and told Rufus that Sheriff Clure had the flu. "He won't be back for a few days," she said. "He's got a pretty good case of it, so I guess our safety's in your hands this week."

"I'll try to take good care of it," Rufus replied.

That afternoon, James Lee Blanton brought his son, Jimmy, to town from Addie, and walked into the sheriff's office with a slightly rusted .30-30 Winchester rifle in the boy's hands.

"Jimmy found this yesterday," James Lee said.

"Where at?"

"I was swimmin' in the Molly Hole in Scotts Creek," Jimmy said, "and I stepped on something hard. It was this rifle."

"The Molly Hole, huh?"

"It's down behind Miss Molly Clayton's house."

"Oh, I know right where it's at," Rufus said. "I been swimmin' a lot of times in it. Is it still deep enough to dive off that big rock?"

"It's deeper than it used to be," Jimmy answered.

"Reckon somebody lost this gun," James Lee said.

"Could be," Rufus answered, "or somebody might'a throwed it in the creek a'purpose to get rid of it. The Molly Hole's about as deep as any hole along there, ain't it still?"

"Yeah, it is," James Lee replied.

"This is interestin'," Rufus said, "very interestin'."

When Jimmy and his dad left, Rufus examined the rifle. Spots of rust were on the barrel. Rufus sighted down the inside of the barrel. He could see his thumbnail at the other end, but he also saw several specks of rust inside the barrel."

"Hmmm," Rufus considered what to do, and finally went around back and came back in with an elongated wash tub that caught rain water from the roof.

He put the rifle in the tub, walked across and down the street to the hardware and bought a gallon of oil. Joe Samples, who owned the store, was not there. The gallon did not cover the rifle in the tub, so he went back and bought two more gallons and added them to the first. That was enough. The oil covered the rifle when the tub was tilted and soaked into the barrel.

"I'll leave that be for a day or two an' see what happens," he said.

Soon Samples came from the hardware store to the sheriff's office to see what Rufus was doing.

"That there is motor oil," Joe said. "It's for cars. It's a lot thicker'n kerosene. Maybe it'll cut that rust out'a the barrel."

"Hope so," Rufus answered. "This might be the break we've been lookin' for. I need to shoot this gun in the box."

"I'd leave it in the oil tonight," Joe said, "and take it out and check it tomorrow. Just run a cloth through the barrel several times to clean out the oil, four or five times if you need to, and maybe a brush to help cut out the rust, then wipe off the whole rifle, including the chamber and the trigger housing and all. After that you might be able to fire it all right—if all the rust is gone from the barrel and it looks clean enough."

"Thanks, Joe," Rufus said. "I appreciate your help."

"Any time, Rufus."

"See you later."

Sheriff Clure was up and around, feeling much better. Rufus stopped by to see him on his way home that evening, and Clure told him, "I feel like going back to work tomorrow. Since it's Saturday, why don't you take the day off and you can watch the office Sunday."

"Thanks," Rufus said. "I hear they're racing some tomorrow down at the fairgrounds. I might go and see who and what's runnin'. Might be the day I'll race Fred."

"Can that mule run?"

"Don't tell nobody," Rufus said, "but he'll outrun most of the horses in this county."

TWENTY-ONE

Saturday morning dawned bright and clear. Rufus looked out the window while eating breakfast and chuckled to himself. "Looks like a good day for racin'." He finished breakfast, climbed into the loft of the house and secured the box in which he kept his money.

Taking it to the table, he called his mother.

"Ma, how 'bout countin' this and see how much money I've got."

She began counting the stack of bills and when she finished, she said, "Rufus, you've got around three hundred dollars in this box, and you need to learn to count, son."

"Good," he said. "I'm a'aimin' to learn. Count me out a hundred."

She laid five twenty dollar bills on the table. Rufus folded them and tucked them in his shirt pocket, buttoning the pocket for safe-keeping.

"How much is one of 'em worth," Rufus asked.

"Twenty dollars," his mother answered.

"An' all together they're worth a hundred?"

"That's right, son, an even hundred."

"Thanks, Ma, I'll be back later," he said, "if I don't run into somethin' else to do. Right now I'm gonna look for a horse to race old Fred against."

"Well, then, good luck," she responded.

At the fairgrounds, Rufus saw a half-dozen horses being readied for the races. One, he noticed was the big Morgan stallion belonging to the Hannessey brothers.

He walked around and looked over the other horses, and not any of them scared him. Fred, he thought, can outrun anything here, less'n it's that Morgan, an' might be she could beat him. I'll think about it a while.

He watched as the Morgan ran in the first race against a beautiful stud belonging to Ham Bailey from Wilmot. The Morgan jumped into an early lead and won the race going away.

"He's a fast runner," Rufus said to himself, "but I reckon Fred could take him. I'd ruther beat them Hannessey boys than anybody here."

He ran his arm around Fred's neck, pulled her head up close and whispered, "What'd you think, Fred?"

Fred did not respond, so Rufus watched a few more races. The Morgan beat some good horse flesh and the Hannessey boys won three or four hundred dollars.

Rufus mounted Fred bareback, of course, and trotted over to the Hannessey horse.

"Pretty fast animal you got there, boys." he said. He looked over the large, very expensive, hand-tooled saddle, then at Tom Hannessey's two hundred pound frame.

"Fast enough," Hannessey said. "Ain't nobody beat him yet."

"Why," Rufus said slowly, "my old mule could outrun *him*."

"You're kidding us!" Tom Hannessey exclaimed, eying the mule, and then began to laugh. "Come on. Let's find somebody to race."

"This mule can outrun your Morgan easy," Rufus baited.

"You want to try?" Hannessey asked.

"Reckon so," Rufus said. "We'll give her a go, if you ain't afraid to run ag'in my mule."

"Afraid?" Hannessey asked, incredulously. "Come on. Show me."

"Tell you what we'll do," Hannessey responded. "We'll spot you a twenty foot start and bet you all you wanna bet we'll outrun you."

"What kinda odds you givin'?" Rufus asked.

"What kind do you want?"

"Oh, I'd say for this distance," Rufus said, eying the hundred yards to the finish line, "about four to one."

"That ain't enough," Hannessey said. "We'll give you an even five to one. How much you wanna bet?"

"Let's see," said Rufus, digging into his shirt pocket and drawing out a twenty-dollar bill. "How 'bout that! I got an even twenty dollars here. I'll just bet it all."

"We'll take it," Hannessey laughed. "We could use another twenty. We ain't won much so far this mornin'."

"Wait a minute," Rufus said. "Derned if I ain't got some more in here." He pretended to dig around in his shirt pocket, and then withdrew the other four twenties.

"Let's just make it an even hundred."

"You got it," Tom said, angrily. "We'll cover the whole hundred. Be the easiest money we've made today."

"Oh, yeah," Rufus added, "an' we don't want no twenty-foot start. We'll just run the whole hundred."

"In that case," Tom Hannessey gloated, "we'll just up the odds to seven to one."

"Well, I don't know," Rufus said. "You seem to be awful sure of your hoss. I don't know whether we ought to do this or not, Fred."

"You can't back out now," Tom said. "You done took the bet."

"Well, all right," Rufus said, trying to sound grudging. "Guess we did say we'd do it."

"You bet you said it," Hannessey said. "Ain't no backin' out."

"All right," Rufus said. "Who holds the money?"

Ted Mull stepped forward. "I'll hold 'er. Gimme your seven hundred, Tom."

Hannessey passed over the money.

Rufus whispered in Fred's ear, "You can take him, Fred. He's a'carryin' at least two hundred and forty pounds."

Hannessey brought the Morgan to the starting line, acting anxious.

"Seems like you're takin' an awful chance," Rufus said to Hannessey, "a'bettin' seven hundred to make one."

"I ain't taking no chance atall," Hannessey said. "Ain't a mule in the world could outrun this horse."

"Ready?" the starter asked, and both riders poised themselves for the start.

The starter raised a pistol in the air, pulled the trigger, and both horse and mule were off like two shots.

Rufus held Fred back for the first twenty yards, letting the Morgan take a seven- or eight-yard lead, and then he freed Fred with the reins, and said to the mule, "Go get 'em, Fred. They're all yours."

The mule laid back her ears and put on a burst of speed and with twenty-five yards to go pulled even with the Morgan.

Hannessey used the whip, lashing brutally at the horse's sides, trying to coax more speed. Rufus just talked to Fred, "Get goin', girl," he said, tapping the mule in the side with his boots. "Come on, lady, eat 'em up!"

Fred gave another burst of speed, pulled away from the Morgan on the fly, and crossed the finish line five yards in the lead.

The crowd began to yell, pleasure written all over them.

"Way to go, Rufus!"

"Yoweee, never seen a mule run like that!"

"What'd you feed him this mornin', Rufe?—Dynamite!"

"Him?" Rufus exclaimed. "Why, this here's a girl mule."

"You ain't tellin' me a little old girl beat that big Morgan?" Sid Frady asked.

"Reckon so," Rufus returned. "Seems to me it did."

They trotted back to the starting line, and Hannessey assaulted Rufus with his mouth. "You cheated, you yellow son of a. ..."

Rufus hit him in the mouth with a big fist, flooring him on the spot.

"Tom," he said, looking down at Hannessey, "I wasn't really gonna race till you opened your big mouth. Some day you'll learn when to keep it shut. An' I'm a'thankin' you for the money. I can use it."

Several of the onlookers gathered round. Ted Mull stepped forward and handed Rufus eight hundred dollars. "You won it fair and square," Ted said. "I've never seen a mule run like that."

"Reckon that's cause you ain't never seen Fred run," Rufus laughed. "Anybody else wanna test this here mule?"

No one answered

"I'm a'thankin' you," Rufus said.

Hannessey turned his back and walked away. The crowd began looking Fred over.

"Well," one man said, "she ain't nothing but a mule, but she's the fastest danged mule I ever seen. I ain't hardly believing what I just witnessed."

Rufus grinned, mounted Fred, and rode from the fairgrounds with eight hundred dollars in his pocket.

When they reached the road, Rufus patted Fred on the shoulder and said, "I guess your racing days are done, girl. Ain't nobody around here gonna give us another run. On second thought, we might go to Waynesville some Saturday an' see what we can do over there."

At home, he handed the money to his mother. "How much do I have now?" he asked.

"Well, let's see," she said. "This here's eight hundred and you've got two hundred left in the box. I reckon you've got a thousand dollars right now."

"A thousand dollars!" he exclaimed. "That's a lot o' money, ain't it?"

"Near 'bout enough to get that whole mountainside cleared of brush and grassed, I guess," she said, "so's you can start raising them horses you wanted to."

"Lord have mercy!" he was thrilled to hear that he had that much. "Ma, I ain't told you yet, but Sue's helpin' me learn to read an' write. When we're finished with that, I'm gonna ask her to teach me how to cipher."

"She can do that," his ma said. "Sue's good at things like that. By the way, you and Sue's getting' pretty thick, ain't you?"

"Reckon we are," Rufus replied. "I don't know what love feels like, but if it feels like I think it does, I'm in love with her."

"I knowed that," his ma said. "How does she feel 'bout it?"

"Seems to feel the same way I do," he said happily. "That's one reason I wanted to learn to read an' write an' count, an' she's a'teachin' me."

Lissa Silver©

TWENTY-TWO

Rufus didn't go to church with Sue that Sunday. Instead, he came in to do duty in the sheriff's office. He checked the rifle soaking in motor oil and saw rust still on it, so he ran a brush through it several times and laid it back in the tub and told himself he'd check it again first thing in the morning.

No one came in with sheriff's business that morning, so he spent his time putting more order to the office. Then he swept and washed a couple of dirty windows and in the afternoon settled back in the big chair behind the desk, propped his feet on the desk, and slept a part of the afternoon.

Going to sleep, he thought of who he would get to clean off the mountainside, removing the blackberry vines and brush. There were no trees to remove, but he did need a fence built around the whole horse pasture, and that would take some time—and some money, but he figured he had enough to go ahead with the job.

When he woke late in the afternoon, he picked up where he had left off and said to himself. "Don't know who I'll get to do the job, but somebody around here could use the work. I'll think of somebody."

Suddenly he thought of the Barker brothers in Beta. "They'll do the job," he said aloud, "an' they'll do it right, too."

He closed and locked the office at six that afternoon, retrieved Fred from the livery stable and headed home. Even though spring was well on its way, the streets were fairly dark at that hour because of a heavy overcast that threatened rain.

As he rode out of the business district, he noticed lamplight shining through the windows of several homes, and when he approached Sue's house on the outskirts of town, he debated whether to stop or ride on to Beta and ask the Barker brothers if they would turn his mountainside into horse pasture. But Fred, of her own inclination, turned in toward Sue's house, and Rufus, chuckling about it, let her have her head.

Fred pulled up at the front porch and Rufus dismounted, dropped the reins in front of Fred and crossed the porch and knocked on the door.

Sue answered, "Why, Rufus. Come in. I'm glad to see you."

"Well, I was thinkin' about riding up to Beta to get the Barker boys to do some work turnin' my mountainside into pastureland," he said, "but Fred turned in here an' I didn't have the heart to turn her back on the road."

"Good!" Sue exclaimed. "I'm glad she knows to stop here. Come on in. I'm just taking supper out of the oven, so you're in time to eat."

"That's right neighborly of you," said Rufus, grinning, "I'd'a stopped too, if I hadn't been thinking hard about seein' the Barkers."

"Doesn't matter why," she said. "I'm glad to see you. I've been thinking about you this afternoon. I'm so pleased with the way you're coming with reading and writing that I wrote some sentences on the blackboard to see if you can read them."

"I'll give 'er a shot," Rufus said. "Let's see 'em."

She led him into the parlor. "Read me that first sentence," she said.

"Okay," Rufus answered, studying the first sentence on the board.

"It says, I. . . . I don't know that next word."

"It's hear, like hearing with your ears. Remember, we went over it last night. H...E...A...R."

"All right," Rufus said. "I hear, uh, th...."

"It's the," she said. "Remember, T...H...E..."

"Oh yeah," he said. "I hear the, uh, dog, uh, uh, a'barkin'."

"No," she said. "You got it right, but you don't say 'A barkin'. It's just 'barking.' Remember, I-N-G, I-N-G, like 'RING,' without the R, and don't say 'a'barkin'.' It's just 'barking.' I-N-G I-N-G, like king without the K."

"I remember," he said. "I hear the dog barking."

"That's good, Rufus, very good. Now read the next one."

He fumbled with a few words, then said, "The cat sat on the porch."

"Great," she said. "You're catching on quickly."

"I could catch on quicker," he said, "if I didn't have so much on my mind."

She let it go at that and asked him to the table. "I'll get you a plate," she said.

After dinner, they talked about church a bit. "Preacher

Snyder asked where you were this morning," she said. "I told him you had to work today."

"Did he give anybody else what for over a little moonshinin'?" he asked.

"No. He didn't even mention it."

"Ah ha!" he exclaimed. "He was just a'talkin' to me."

"No, Rufus, he wasn't *a'talkin'* to you. He was *talking* to you. Talking! Talking! Not a'talkin'."

"I'll try to remember that," he said, "but you keep after me. I want to learn to talk good, so straighten me out when I say something wrong. You won't hurt my feelings."

"I will, I promise," Sue said beaming. She was proud of Rufus. Anyone could see that.

Rufus rode on home after supper. "Makes me tireder a'doin' nothin'," he said to his mother, "than it does a...uh, doing a whole lot." He pronounced the last four words slowly and carefully."

"You're a'learnin', son," she said. "Keep it up."

"I will, Ma. I'll see you in the mornin'."

TWENTY-THREE

Monday morning was usually a fairly slow time in the Sheriff's Department. Most of those who came in were holding their heads from heavy hangovers. Rufus unlocked the door at eight and went in. He immediately began to clean up yesterday's clutter. He carried out the trash and dumped it, swept the floor, straightened up the mess of papers on the desk, and then dried off the soaking rifle and swabbed out the barrel.

Looking down the barrel, he saw no remaining rust. The firing mechanism worked smoothly, so he took a shell out of a box and carried the rifle outside. Looking across the street, he saw Velt Wilson outside his café getting a breath of fresh air.

"Hey, Velt, come over here a minute."

Velt crossed the street and followed Rufus to the rear of the office. There Rufus loaded the shell in the rifle, aimed into the box, and pulled the trigger. The rifle fired like a new one. He placed the gun aside and dug down in the sand, found the bullet, and removed it.

"Now come in the office with me," he told Velt. "I'm gonna check this round under a microscope and if it matches, I want you to look in the scope and see it so's you can witness what I done.

"Remember," he said emphatically to Velt, "that you saw

me take this bullet out of the sack labeled MOLLY HOLE and place it under the microscope, and that this is the one I just fired from this gun."

"I will," Velt said. "I'll remember that." He watched closely as Rufus placed the second round under the microscope.

Peering into the eyepiece, Rufus rolled the bullet he had just fired until he saw the markings matched the ones on the other.

"Ah ha!" he exclaimed. "Perfect match. Look in here, Velt, and study both bullets. See if you can tell any difference. The one on the right is the bullet that was fired through Sid's heart after he was already dead."

Velt eyed the two rounds for half a minute and then said, "Looks like a perfect match to me."

"We may need you to testify in court that you saw me shoot this bullet into the barrel and that these bullets matched," Rufus said. "If we ever find the man who owned this gun, we'll be on the way to clearing up this case."

"I'll be glad to do that," Velt said. "Need to get that man out of circulation. I didn't know you could write, Rufus."

"I'm learning," Rufus said and felt his chest begin to swell.

Velt said, "I'd better get back to my cooking. Takes a while to get dinner ready in a restaurant."

"By the way, Velt, don't mention this to nobody."

"Oh, I won't," he said and left.

Rufus placed the rifle on the desk.

"Won't say nothin' to nobody 'bout this 'cept the sheriff," he said. "Might reach the wrong ears. All we got to do now is find out whose rifle this is, an' that ain't gonna be easy. But, by George, we'll find him or my name ain't Rufus Raby."

Later, Clure stopped by to see that all was going well, and Rufus had him look at the rounds under the scope. "Perfect match," Clure said. "Whoever had that rifle knows who killed Sid. Now we just have to find him."

"I don't think it was anybody around Addie," Rufe said. "Somebody from somewhere else throwed it in the creek," and the sheriff agreed.

"Tomorrow morning," the sheriff said, "I want you to take the automobile to Balsam and start asking around if anybody knows somebody who didn't have his rifle fired, and then keep talking to them and maybe you can come up with something. Then come down the mountain and ask around Mount Pleasant and Willits.

"We won't get any more rifles out of this," he said, "but you might come up with a lead of some sort, or at least another angle we haven't thought of."

Lisey Silver©

TWENTY-FOUR

Tuesday dawned a beautiful spring day. Rufus thought about asking Sue to ride with him but decided against it. He could take her along some other time; wasn't no tellin' what he might run into on this trip.

In Balsam, a mountain community that sat astride the road from Sylva to Waynesville at the Jackson-Haywood county line, Rufus began to inquire again at each house if the people knew anyone who had a .30-30 that hadn't been tested. He didn't expect everyone—nor even anyone—to respond as they had the first time. People were reluctant to give information of that sort about neighbors, particularly when murder was involved. To most mountain people, questions of that nature smacked of suspicion and folks in the mountains were clannish and shut-mouthed when it came to giving incriminating information on a neighbor, especially if they suspected the neighbor had something to do with the crime. They simply locked their doors at night and asked the Lord to look after them till morning.

There was always a chance, Rufus thought. Someone sometimes talked, provided immunity was granted. He came to Samson Reed's home, knocked on the door, and Reed invited him in.

"Ain't got time," Rufus answered. "You got a .30-30 rifle?"

"Yes, I have," Reed responded. "Why?"

"Need to borrow it," Rufus said. "We're test-firin' every thirty caliber in the county an' I missed some up here the first time."

"Is this about Sid?" Reed asked. "Thought he was killed by a blow on the head."

"He was. But after he died, somebody shot him through the heart with a thirty caliber rifle."

"Come on in," Reed said, "I'll get mine."

Moments later, he handed Rufus a new .30-30 Winchester. "Ain't never been shot," Reed said. "Just bought it day before yesterday."

"What happened to your old one?"

"Sold it to a feller for forty dollars, then got this new one for sixty. Figured I come out on the deal."

"Where'd you buy this one?"

"At the hardware in Waynesville."

"Who'd you sell the old one to?"

"Never got the feller's name; don't believe he even give it to me. Didn't matter no way."

"You didn't know him?"

"No, I didn't."

"Ever see him before?"

"Nope. Total stranger."

"Strange to me you didn't ask his name."

"Nothin' to make out of that, Rufe. His name didn't matter. I was just interested in makin' a good swap."

"Thanks," Rufus said. "Don't think we'll need to shoot this gun, seeing how it's brand new and you didn't have it when Sid was killed."

To himself, Rufus said, "That'll smoke him out if he's the one." He cranked the Model-T and drove back down the long, dusty way to the main road. There, out of sight of Reed's house, he turned toward Waynesville. Arriving in that town, he pulled up and parked in front of the Waynesville Hardware.

Rufus identified himself to the clerk and showed his badge. Then he asked the clerk, "Did Samson Reed buy a rifle here?"

The clerk checked the store's books, and said, "Sure did. He bought it day before yesterday. Sixty dollars. It was a .30-30 Winchester."

"Did you see him sell his old one?"

"His old one?" the clerk asked. "No, he didn't trade one in. He didn't even have an old one with him when he come in."

Rufus thanked him and left. "Danged if that ain't a brick wall," he said.

Back in Sylva, Rufus told Samson Reed's story to the sheriff.

"Well, that's not suspicious," said Clure, back on the job after his bout with the flu, "but is sure is strange, coming at exactly this time. Our best lead is this rifle in the tub. Maybe you can show it to his friends around the county and ask if they recognize it without raising suspicion with anybody. I'd guess he didn't sell it to anybody, and he could have been the one who threw his rifle in the creek. He came all the way down to Addie to throw off suspicion—if he did do it. That's about eight miles. You may be onto something,

Rufus, but I don't yet know if we can put it to use. Just stay on it. A man wouldn't throw a perfectly good Winchester in the creek for nothing. I'd say you're on a track of some kind; stick to it!"

"I'll stay on it, John. It's on my mind that the prime suspects in this case right now are the Hannessey boys and Samson Reed.

"But Samson would have had outside help to carry Sid's body up the mountain and help him get it in the rattlesnake den, even if he is a big, strong man," said Clure. "That would'a been tricky business at best, and it seems to me that a man of any size and strength would need help doing that."

"Besides, we already talked about this once," Rufus responded. "Remember I told you about stuffing wading boots, and if the plank was long enough, it could be done."

"Rufus, you've got to put your mind to rest for a while. Take the afternoon off and try to get your mind off the case. Why don't you take Sue for a ride?" the sheriff offered. "Take the car. She'd enjoy it. Has she ever ridden in a car before?"

"I don't know," Rufus answered. "I'll find out."

Then I'll see you tomorrow morning. I'll be late coming in, so you open up and get things rolling. When I get here you can go and investigate some more. I should be in by noon."

With a girl-like exuberance, Sue was overjoyed that Rufus was taking her for a ride. "I've sat in a car before," she said, "but have never ridden in one."

Beside the Tuckaseigee they rode to Cullowhee. Sue sat stiffly in the front seat with Rufus, holding on to the door, amazed at how fast they were going. In Cullowhee, they drove slowly around some of the campus of the school that Professor Madison had founded.

"Some of the professor's folks still live in Sylva," Rufus said, making conversation.

Trails twisted all through the campus. No one had automobiles, and the trails were foot paths.

"Let's just park the car and walk around," Rufus suggested.

They spent an hour looking over the campus, sitting by a water fountain for much of the hour. The fountain shot a spray of water twenty feet in the air, and it was beautiful.

Students wandered about; some hurried to classes. While Sue and Rufus sat by the fountain, other couples came by and sat on the grass.

Sue whispered to Rufus, "Some of these kids are in love. You can tell it by their eyes, by the way they look at each other." For a while, then, Rufus tried to avoid looking directly at Sue, fearing she might read something in his own eyes, and he wasn't yet sure exactly what it was—but he had his suspicions.

The afternoon was late when they returned to the automobile. Rufus cranked it, and thirty minutes later they were back at Sue's house.

"Come on in," she invited. "I'll fix supper."

"Thanks, but I better get this car back to the office."

"Go ahead. I'll start cooking."

"I'll ride Fred back."

Rufus spent the next two weeks asking men all over the county if they knew who owned the rifle. It had distinctive wood grain markings on the stock. No one, however, recognized it. When he came to town one afternoon, Samson Reed himself looked at the rifle, studied the stock and seemed to pale a bit, Rufus thought. He handed the weapon back to Rufus. His breathing was a bit thinner, Rufus noticed, but he said he'd never seen the rifle.

Later, to see what reaction he would get, Rufus showed the rifle to some of Reed's friends at Balsam, not any of whom admitted to recognizing it.

One of Reed's friends, Harley Woodson, did a double take when he saw the gun, but looked it over, shook his head, and handed it back to Rufus. "I've seen that rifle somewheres," Woodson said, "but I don't remember where. If I remember, I'll get in touch." He quickly walked away, his face ashen.

Spring was turning into summer when Rufus finished searching for someone who might identify the rifle. Rufus worked in his fields from quitting time in the office until total darkness. His crops were up and growing and he had to tend to weeding and hoeing. He liked to start those jobs early, keeping his fields clean.

The weather was beautiful, except the day he and Sue rode their mounts a half-mile up the creek above Rufus's house where the road played out in a wall of forest. Sue had prepared a picnic supper. They sat in a forest glade enjoying it and certainly enjoying each other's company. Suddenly Rufus felt a drop of water on his wrist.

"Hut, oh," he said to Sue, and another drop fell on his forehead. "It's goin' to rain. I thought it was getting mighty dark."

The shower came swiftly around the mountainside in a gray sheet of falling water that Sue thought was beautiful, but it soaked them to the skin before they reached his house. Sue's hair clung wetly to her head and back, even though Rufus had shed his shirt and put it over Sue's head and shoulders. The shirt was drenched.

They laughed all the way to Rufus's house, where his mother helped Sue dry her hair and made her remove her drenched clothing and put on a heavy robe.

"Build a fire, Rufus," his mother ordered, and soon a couple of small poplar logs hissed and popped in the fireplace.

"Reckon you better stay the night, Sue," Rufus's mother said, and Sue spent that night sleeping soundly in Rufus's departed brother's bed, lying on a mattress stuffed with corn shucks. She had slept on shucks before at her Aunt Mamie's house, and the bed was comfortable once she moved the butt ends of the shucks around so they didn't stick. She did the same at Rufus's house and slept like a baby. She had not realized how tired she was.

Rain from a strong spring shower pounded on the tin roof for an hour or more, but it was like music to Rufus, who thought how much it would help his crops.

For a long while, Rufus sat in a chair by the fire, surprising himself by not thinking about Sue sleeping so near.

His mind was filled with Hannesseys and Samson Reed, and Balsam people.

He talked to himself, keeping his voice low so he wouldn't wake Sue or his mother.

Rufus worried that the case of Sid's murder might not ever be solved.

"Up till now," he told himself, "I've felt like a cub bear playing with his pud. I need to get on track and put some thinkin' into it and see what I'm missing. There's something there that I'm not seeing. I'm not doing a good job and I know it. Wish I knew more. I owe it to Sid."

What could he do that he wasn't already doing? So far, he thought he was doing all he could, but there was a missing link. He knew he had to take a different approach. But what?

He dozed for a while, sitting in his rocking chair, and when he awakened the fire had almost burned down. He put on a couple more sticks of poplar and settled back to think amidst the comforting popping and crackling of the fire.

Again he dozed and when he woke, he started to go to bed, but suddenly he came wide awake. "There is something I can do," he said to himself. "Maybe I need to put a little more bait on the hook. I'll think about it tomorrow. I'm too tired right now." He looked at the clock on the mantle and saw that it was a quarter to midnight.

He heaved himself out of the chair, walked to his room, peeled down to his underwear and crawled into bed, which also had a mattress bag filled with corn shucks but instantly he was asleep, thinking he would put his mind to a test tomorrow.

But he didn't wait until the morrow. In his sleep, his mind held to the subject, and he dreamed of the rifle lying in the oil in the sheriff's office. Some time later, he dreamed of the oil in the pan again, but this time there was no rifle. Save for the oil, the tub was empty.

He awakened with a start! Where's the rifle? What happened to that rifle?

Then he fell on the pillow and his mind was instantly enwrapped in a deep sleep. He dreamed of the Hannessey boys, but the dream was disjointed and not clear in his mind. He did not wake until his mother called him to breakfast.

Sue was already at the table, looking very pretty with her long black hair, dried and brushed down her back. Despite his mother's presence, Sue was so rapturous looking that he walked to the far end of the table and said, "Good morning, Sue. You are beautiful in the early morning."

He leaned over and kissed her on the forehead, and she smiled broadly at Rufus's mom, who beamed with pride.

"Did you sleep well, Rufus?" Sue asked.

"Well, I slept off an' on," he answered. "Sometimes I was sound asleep and sometimes something was runnin' through my mind. I still don't have no handle on what it was, but I dreamed about that pan of oil in the sheriff's department with the rifle in it and then I dreamed about it again and the rifle wasn't in the tub. I don't know why? Then I dreamed about them Hannessey boys and they was wearing halos." Something snapped in his mind; he hadn't noticed the halos in the dream, but they were there now.

"I know there's something there, but I can't figure out what. I don't get what the halos was for," he said, "but all three of 'em was wearing them. Maybe they're gonna die soon. That's all I can figure."

"Why don't you go over to Granny Nation's house?" Rufus's mother asked. "She could tell you what the dream meant."

"Might do that," he said.

They finished breakfast talking about everything but his dreams. Sue knew he was wrestling with something from his dreams, but could not help him determine what.

What he wrestled with was going to see Granny Nations. He didn't want to go. He thought what she did was witchcraft, and he didn't want any part of it. Too, he wanted to solve this case himself.

"It'll come to you, Rufe. Just relax. Find something else to do today and soon you'll remember what it was you wanted to think about."

Rufus was thinking about what Sue had said when they heard the tramp of feet on the front porch and someone knocked loudly on the door.

"I'll see who it is," Rufus's mom said, rising from her chair and trudging to the door.

A moment later, she returned. "It's the Barker boys, Rufus. They've come to start work on your pasture."

"Good," Rufus said, rising. "Sue, stick around for a while and when I finish with the boys I'll take you home."

TWENTY-FIVE

After shaking hands with the Barker brothers, Sheep, Possum, and Rabbit, he took an hour explaining what he wanted done.

"Boys," he said. "I want the pasture fenced off all the way around. Make it a pole and bob wire fence, and there's a lot of timber about the right size for fence posts up toward the top of the mountain—above the Old Field. Some of it ought'a be cleared off anyway. You can use all of that timber it takes for the job. That'll clear off a lot of grazing land. But don't get into either one of my poplar groves to do any cutting.

"Be very careful when you clean off the Old Field up yonder. I've killed copperheads in that field. There's a rock pile there that needs to be done away with because that's where the snakes live. Don't get in the rock pile. You can probably pull the rocks off the pile with a hoe, but keep your distance. They'll crawl out after you. Once them rocks begin to move, they'll be a mad bunch of snakes. Kill 'em all.

"I was picking blackberries up there last summer and picked over toward the rock pile because that was where the big berries was and I thought I'd top off my bucket with them.

"One of my dogs, Old Sailor, who likes to swim in the creek, was with me, and he kept pulling at my pants legs, trying to pull me away from the rock pile. When I got close to the rocks, he came by me and jumped in the rocks and came back out with a copperhead hanging from his upper lip. He shook it off and I killed it. He took off for home. When I got down there, Ma was putting Watkins linament on the snake bite. The dog disappeared after she finished and we didn't see him again for five days. He come trotting home that sixth morning sound as a dollar. The swelling was gone and he seemed darn happy to be back.

"Now, back to what I want you to do. Run the fence from the road down here along the property line to the top of the mountain, then along the top and bring it down about fifty yards this side of Possum Branch up yonder. That'll make it something of a square.

"After you get the pasture fenced, I want you to build a big pole corral behind a new barn I'll tell you about in a minute. I want the corral made just like the other, only a lot bigger, and use poplar for the posts. There's plenty of it on the property. I'll show you exactly where I want you to cut it. I'll even stake it out for you."

"That's a big job, Rufus," Sheep Barker said, eyeing the extent of the mountain land Rufus wanted turned into a horse pasture. "It'll take a while just to fence it. What else do you want done?"

"I want that mountain cleared off," Rufus said. "Not the poplar groves. Leave them like they are, only clean out all the stuff in them that ain't supposed to be there. Then dig out about fifty of the blackberry vines on the hillside, and bring good root balls with them so's you can take 'em up the creek a ways and put 'em back in the ground on level land on the far side of that two-acre field. Space 'em far enough so we can walk between 'em without getting stuck. I want to grow hay on this side from the vines to the little barn. Put the blackberries on the far side pretty near Possom Branch.

"Then cut all the other brush off the mountain and burn it. After that, haul off all the rocks you can from the pasture and put 'em along Possum Branch. That'll make the creek prettier."

"And then?" Sheep asked.

"When you're finished with that, we'll buy some fertilizer and good grass seed at the hardware and spread it over the pasture. I want good grazing for my horses."

"Is that all?" Sheep asked.

"No," Rufus said, his mind running ahead. "Can you build a barn? My barn ain't fixed to hold horses. It's full now, with my three animals. I told you we'll need a new barn for the horses. We'll build a simple but sturdy and dry horse barn over there where the ground flattens out between the mountain and Possum Branch."

"We can build a barn," Sheep said. "We've built 'em before. How big a barn do you want?"

"One that'll hold twenty horses in stalls. We'll build it facing the creek with the pole corral behind it. In the barn, I want a big, high loft that'll hold plenty of hay. I want a tack room downstairs, and make it big enough for a coupl'a cots in it besides all the tack." Rufus bared his plans. "I'm gonna raise a lot of horses on that land and I want a barn that'll hold at least twenty at a time."

"That's a lotta work," Sheep intoned, studying the mountainside and the land where the barn lot would be built. "We may have to find somebody else to build the barn," he said, "especially if you want this job done in a hurry."

"I want the horse lot to take in part of Possum Branch," Rufus said. "The branch comes out of the ground 'bout half-way up the mountain, and don't run far till it comes into Fisher Creek. It makes a long bend towards the pasture over there where the land flattens out from the hillside and we can build the corral far enough out that way that we can drain some of the branch into the lot. I don't think it'll ever flood enough to damage the barn or corral. That'll give the horses fresh drinking water."

"Say," he said, "I want you boys to study how I put that pole corral together down at the old barn, and we'll build the bigger one like it, with skinned poplar poles, right here behind the horse barn, then we'll bring some of the branch water over to it and corner it through the corral. I'll show you where and how.

"And on second thought," Rufus said, "don't put the rocks I told you to put near Possum Branch. Instead we'll use them to line the channel to the corral."

"How'll we direct the branch from the barn back to the creek?" Sheep asked.

"Been thinking about that," Rufus said. "We'll just turn it back into the branch from where it comes out of the corral. What I'm saying is we'll just let the water from the canal run across the back side of the corral and back into the branch.

"Danged if you ain't plannin' to build this place up," Sheep said, a satisfied grin on his face, thinking of all the work he and his two brothers would have to do—and the money they would make doing it.

"You can get busy any time you want to," Rufus said. "You can start today if you'd like."

"We'll be here early in the morning," Sheep Barker said, "and we'll do you a good job, Rufus."

"I know you will," Rufus answered. "That's why I picked you for the job. Now let's talk about money. Give me a price."

Sheep eyed the mountain and shook his head.

"Reckon that'll be enough hard work to ask at least fifteen dollars a week," he said. "That's fifteen for me and fifteen for each of my brothers."

Quickly, Rufus figured the thousand he had would make a good start on the project. He said to himself, "Maybe can't do all of the job immediately, but I'll use the forty I make a month workin' for the sheriff, and maybe make some more racing Fred in Haywood County, and maybe in Transylvania and Macon and other counties nearby. Might even be able to make enough racing to pay for the whole shebang. But if I can't, there's always my business on Possum Branch. Reckon I could double production for a while and pay off the whole thing with the fruit of the vine."

To Sheep Barker he extended his hand and said, "That's a deal. You can start tomorrow. I'll mark all the days you work on the calendar and pay you accordingly every week."

Sheep shook Rufus's hand. "Obliged," he said. "We was beginning to think we'd have to go to some other county and get jobs, but this'un'll keep us busy till the weather turns cold again." He had been doing some figuring in his head, too.

TWENTY-SIX

The Sheriff's Department in Sylva was a single room the size of two living rooms in a large house. It ran front to back from Main Street to the rear alley. Because the jail was located in the Court House atop the steep Court House Hill at the western end of Main Street, all the space in the downtown sheriff's office belonged to Sheriff Clure and Deputy Raby. That gave the sheriff and deputy all the room they needed for miscellaneous storage or activity with some left over.

The only door to the office was on the east side of the building. Windows gave views of Main Street in front of the office and toward the east.

The office was primitive. The lock on the door was a sizeable padlock hanging outside for which only Sheriff Clure and Rufus had keys. They knew the lock could be prised off easily with a crowbar, but they would have to get along with the lock until the county saw fit to approve a new and stronger door with built-in lock.

The walls of the office were solid, built with brick, and the only way to get through a wall was with a sledge hammer and a lot of muscle and noise. That entry would have to be made from the alley behind the stores and the office. The only other way to jimmy the lock was to knock it off with a hammer, but that would also create noise, and across

Main Street several of the buildings had occupied apartments on the upper floors, so that left the crowbar as the best means of illegal entry.

Rufus thought about the padlock for a couple of days. Late the following afternoon he went across the street for coffee at Velt's. When he returned to the office, the sheriff was gone. Rufus examined the lock closely to prove that anyone could break it off the door and help themselves to anything they wanted in the sheriff's department.

That worried him. He waited until full dark to leave for home, and when he left, he took the rifle from the tub, dried it off, took the little bags holding the matching bullets and pocketed them, and walked over to the horse lot, avoiding the lantern burning at the stable door. He put the bridle on Fred, and climbed aboard. Holding the rifle snugly under his leg against Fred's side, he rode out of town without detection.

When he reached home, he crawled across the rafters over the downstairs rooms and hid the rifle and the bullets in a corner of the attic above his bedroom.

He went to sleep with a smile on his face, thinking of Sue, how pretty she was, how she catered to him, feeding him every time he came by, and spending so much time teaching him to read and write and count—and especially to talk. She had told him that his speech was much improved, but to keep thinking as he spoke and make sure he used proper grammar.

Thinking how hard he was trying to do the things Sue taught him, he went to sleep and slept until morning when his mother woke him and told him he had to be at work by eight o'clock.

He rose, splashed water on his face, shaved, donned his apparel, and put his loaded gun belt around his hips with the butt of the forty-five within easy reach of his right hand. Then he ate breakfast.

Hatless, even though rain threatened from the darkened clouds above, he climbed onto Fred's back, turned him onto the Fisher Creek road and headed for town.

Lissa Silver

TWENTY-SEVEN

At eight in the morning, Sylva was quiet with mostly storekeepers about. Customers would arrive soon. Rufus put Fred in the stable lot, removed the halter from her head, tossed some oats in the trough, and walked on to the office, speaking a good morning to the storekeepers on the street.

He did not notice the damage to the office door until he reached for the handle. The door lock and all of its mechanism lay at his feet, prised off, probably with a crowbar. The door opened with a push and he stepped inside into a puddle of oil.

There was no litter on the floor, the desk had not been ransacked, but his tub of oil had been overturned and run into a great puddle, covering much of the wooden floorboards.

No doubt some of the oil had seeped between the boards, but it would do no harm. There was no basement in the building.

Nothing was missing that Rufus could tell. The four rifles stood in their case, and the furniture and filing cabinets were undisturbed.

Someone had broken in with a single purpose in mind: to take the rifle from the oil tub.

Suddenly, the memory of his dream came to his mind.

He had seen the rifle in the tub, and later had seen the tub with the rifle missing.

"My goodness!" he intoned. "The Lord shore does work in mysterious ways. He told me I'd better take that rifle home with me. He spoke to me in that dream. But what I didn't understand was them halos he showed me on the Hannessey boys' heads."

That afternoon, he came to a realization. Rufus was so impressed by Sheriff Clure's constant reminders to not allow emotions to rule over good judgment, that that began to straighten out his jumbled thinking. At that moment, the thought entered his mind that he had *wanted* the Hannessey boys to be guilty, and that stopped him in his tracks. He had put the cart before the horse. He *had* wanted them to be guilty.

When Sheriff Clure came to work half an hour later, he was concerned that the murder rifle was gone until Rufus told him of his dream and how he had taken the rifle and the bullets home with him and had hidden them in his attic.

"That's good thinking, Rufus," Clure congratulated him. "Don't tell anyone that we have the rifle, not even your mother. Now come on, we'll spread out this oil and use it to preserve the floor."

For the remainder of the day, they swept oil into corners, spread it all over the floor, and worked it into the wood.

In the afternoon, county workmen arrived and replaced the old door with a new, more sturdy one that had a strong, built-in locking mechanism. Clure and Rufus each took a key to the new door, and when they were ready to leave, Sheriff Clure said to Rufus, "Go home, Rufe, and don't think about any of this. Get your mind off it. Take Sue to dinner. Relax. You're beginning to think like a detective. Encourage those thoughts and we'll beat 'em at their own game, but relax your mind for a while. Give it a chance to rest."

Rufus was lost in thought all the way home. He let Fred pick her route and when he reached the farm, he put Fred in a stall, had dinner with his mother, then told her that he would be gone the remainder of the night.

"Be careful, son," Paralee said. "You've got a'hold of somethin' that you can't turn loose till you've solved it, and I'm a'thinkin' that you'll work it out in your mind in your own way. You'll be a better man for all of this. I know that'll happen."

"I'm going camping," Rufus said to his mother. "I'm just going up the pasture hill, build a fire, do some chewin' an' spittin' in the fire, and try to think this thing out. I'll see you in time for breakfast in the mornin'."

Halfway up the mountainside, perhaps two hundred yards from the barn and corral, Rufus chose a level spot and built a fire. He unrolled his bedroll and laid it beside the fire, then took a lusty bite of a tobacco twist and settled down to do some serious chewing and spitting."

After darkness fell, Rufus was surprised to see a flicker of light moving toward him from the barn. "That's somebody with a lantern," he said, watching the light bob.

Nearing the camp, Rufus recognized his visitor as Sue. "Come on in, Sue;" he said. "Maybe you'd like to chew an' spit a little with me."

"We'd both probably put out the fire," she laughed, knowing that he knew she did not chew, as some mountain women did, even at her age. She sat beside him, gazing into the flames.

"Rufus," she said, "it seems to me you're troubled.

"Reckon so," he answered. "You know I'm troubled. This whole thing is about to buffalo me."

"What do you mean?"

"I mean in my mind I've probably sinned. I've convicted the Hannessey boys of something they might not be guilty of. The sheriff tried to caution me and he was right all along. I've been wrong. The Hannesseys might not be any guiltier than you are, but I have already convicted them simply because I *wanted* them to be guilty. That is not the way the law works.

"When I dreamed they were wearing halos, I jumped to the conclusion that they were gonna die soon," he added, "but that isn't it. Maybe it meant something else."

"I can think of but one other thing," Sue said. "Maybe it meant that they're not guilty at all."

Rufus pondered that.

Slowly he said, "You've give me a powerful lot to be thinking about. I need to go see Ralph Farmer. He was the only one who saw my brother killed and it's about time I got the straight of that killing, I reckon."

"May I come with you? Perhaps I could help you."

"Yes, I want you to."

As his name implied, Ralph Farmer was indeed a farmer. He owned a sidehill farm, a hundred-sixty acres of good ground a mile up Barker's Creek from the Tuckaseigee River at Wilmot.

"We'll take the car and go see him in the morning," Rufus said. "We can get there from Sylva in about thirty minutes, so why don't we leave about ten?"

"I'm glad," she said, looking at him admiringly. "You're thinking straight and I believe your mind is open to possibilities."

The following morning about eleven o'clock, Sue, Rufus, and Ralph Farmer sat on the side of Barker's Creek, watching the small stream chuckle over its rocky bed.

"I was in the woods right over there," Farmer indicated the place with a point of his chin. "Me and Bertha Nations was going for a walk and was out of sight of your brother and the Hannesseys, but we could see him and them. I'm a'goin' to tell you what I seen an' how come I seen it. Tom Hannessey and your brother were both sweet on Bertha, so we laid low, didn't want either one of them to see us. I wouldn't'a stood a chance against either one of 'em, let alone both.

"Your brother seemed like he wanted to fight. I dunno why he'd pick it with all three. Them was right bad odds. I heard William tell Tom that he thought he ought to just shoot him, and when I heard that I shore enough didn't want them to see Bertha and me together.

"That's when I thought about runnin', Bertha or no

Bertha. Reckon I figured she could take care of herself, not in a man's fight, o'course, but in her own way."

"Ralph, I want you to tell me what went on between my brother and the Hannesseys, and give it to me straight. I don't want you to pull any punches but tell me exactly what you saw. That could mean a lot to me."

"All right, Rufus; I done told you that William was right belligerent an' it wasn't only Tom he threatened to shoot. He threatened all three of 'em, an' I guess William come prepared. He was armed and he pulled his gun.

"I'd have to say William was shot in self defense, 'cause him and Tom went for their guns about the same time. It was a simple fact that Tom got in action first an' shot William through the heart. When we saw that William was dead, me an' Bertha beat it. They didn't see us go; I guess they was so shocked. We run all the way to my house.

"Rufus, I'd appreciate it if you'd keep us out of it, Bertha anyway."

"Far as I'm concerned," Rufus said. "I won't get either one of you in it, 'cause this conversation was for my own benefit, not for the law's. I've been thinking that William was murdered, but according to what you've told me, it wasn't murder."

"Nope! Least, I didn't see it thataway. It was purely a case of self defense. That may be hard for you to swallow, but that's the way I seen it."

TWENTY-EIGHT

When Rufus reported for work the next morning, Sheriff Clure said, "Lock the door, Rufe."

"Lock the door? Why?"

"We need to talk. I want to go over what we've got and what we need and see where to go from here."

Rufus locked the door and pulled the shades.

"That tight enough for you?" he asked.

"That's good. Sit down."

"Wait a minute," Rufus offered. "Let me start some coffee."

When the water began to boil, Rufus tossed a handful of coffee into the pot.

"Okay," said the sheriff. "Where are we?"

"We're in Sylva!" Rufe said with tongue in cheek.

The sheriff laughed. "Be serious."

"Okay. Well, let's see," Rufus said. "We know we're looking for a big-footed man. That was our first lead."

"And it wasn't a lead at all," Clure responded. "Half the men in this county are big-footed."

"You're right about that," Rufus said. "Where to now?"

"We've got the rifle and the matching slugs," Clure said, "but they don't do us any good till we find who owned the gun. What else?"

"We're running out of suspects," Rufus said. "I've eliminated the Hannessey boys from that list."

"How come?"

"Talked to Ralph Farmer yesterday. He's the only one who saw William killed. I asked him to level with me, to forget that William was my brother and tell me everything he saw and heard. He said William instigated the argument with the Hannesseys and if he was called on the witness stand he'd have to swear that the killing of William was a matter of self-defense. Just like you said it was.

"I asked him to let the chips fall where they may. The way he told me what happened, danged if I wouldn't have to agree with him."

"Why?"

"Well, my brother was given to fits of anger, and since him and Tom Hannessey had been running after Bertha Nations, I can see how William might fly off the handle and pitch a little fit. Maybe not enough to get killed for, but that's how it turned out."

"So that would eliminate the Hannesseys."

"Way I see it," Rufus said, "it probably would—unless something else comes up—and I have to agree with Ralph. I think he was telling me the truth. That was the way he saw it and that's about the way my brother was, belligerent, I think Ralph called him."

"Can't argue too much with that," Clure said thoughtfully.

"I don't think now that the Hannesseys could be cold-blooded killers, so, the way I'm looking at it is we only have one more lead," Rufus said.

"I don't follow you. What lead?"

"My latest gut feeling!"

"And what's that?"

Rufus told him about the reaction of Harley Woodson when he showed him the rifle. "He knew whose gun it was," Rufus said. "He turned pale as a ghost. He knew, all right. And he got away from there like a scalded cat so's he wouldn't have to finger Samson Reed. Samson's a dangerous bully, given to fits of anger. And remember Reed was at that card game when Sid won the six hundred dollars."

"Don't forget that your gut reactions have turned up a big zero so far," the sheriff said.

"I know it," Rufus replied, "and I know why. It was because I *wanted* the Hannesseys to be guilty. I can see that now that my eyes are wide open. Sue saw it, too."

"So how can we get the truth—if it is the truth—out of Harley Woodson now?"

"I have an idea, and I believe it'll work."

"Tell me."

"Harley's been out of work for a month or two. You think you can wheedle a hundred dollars reward money out of the commissioners for information leading to the arrest and conviction of the killers?"

"Doubt it," Clure said. "Might get 'em to kick in fifty."

"That won't sweeten the pot enough," Rufus said. "Any man who's going down for the third time will grab at a hundred dollar bill. I have a feeling that a hundred will work, but I'm not sure fifty will."

"Well, it's true," mused the sheriff, "that we don't have anything else to go on. If this don't pan out, the killers might get off scot free."

"I really feel this'll work," Rufus said. "It just has to. Way I see it, it's the only chance we've got."

"Yeah," Clure replied, "and if it don't, we'll be up the creek without a paddle."

"I'll make it work," Rufus stated flatly.

"No, no, Rufus! No strong-arm stuff."

"Not thinking that way," Rufus said. "Got an idea how to make it work."

"It better be good—and legal, too," the sheriff said. "Meet me back here about dinner time."

"All right," Rufus responded. "I'll see you here then. And get the money in cash. That's important."

They locked the office. In the Model T, Clure headed for the Court House on the hill and Rufus boarded Fred and turned her toward Fisher Creek.

An hour later, Rufus rode into the front yard of the farm, ground hitched Fred and went in the house.

"You're home early, Rufus," his mother said. "I ain't even started dinner."

"No time to eat, anyway," he said. "I'll get the box and I want you to count me out fifty dollars."

"That's a lot of money," she said. "What's it for?"

"It's just money I need," Rufus said. "Got an idea how it can help me solve Sid's murder case."

"How?"

"Don't ask any more questions, Ma. And don't say a word about this to nobody. I mean nobody. That might knock the pins out from under our last chance to find the guilty party."

Fifteen minutes later, astride Fred, Rufus headed back to Sylva with fifty dollars in his pocket.

He met Clure at the office at noon and Clure gave him fifty in cash.

"I hope that's enough," the sheriff said. "I almost had to get down on my knees and beg for it."

"It'll be enough," Rufus said. He went across the street to the bank and changed the money in his pocket for a hundred dollar bill.

Lissa Silver©

TWENTY-NINE

"By the way, sheriff," Rufus said when he returned from the bank, "mind telling me what that funny-looking contraption is hanging on the wall?" Rufus asked, staring at an oaken box with a round tube embedded in the front of the box and a small crank on the right side.

"Why, that's one of those new-fangled telephones," Clure answered. "They installed it this morning while we were gone. It's connected to the railroad lines that run alongside the tracks. When nobody else is using it, you can talk through that tube, holding the wired contraption on the left side to your ear and I'll guarantee you they can hear you all the way to Waynesville.

"There's one here, one in the depot, and another in the court house. Then they've put one in a home in Addie, one in Willits, another in Balsam, and some in Waynesville. You can talk to any one in any of them places by giving the Waynesville operator a number off that card on the wall. That way we can maintain better touch along the line. It's new-fangled, but it works! They'll make manhunting a whole lot easier when we all learn to use them, so pay attention to the sheet of numbers tacked to the wall."

"What'll they think of next?" Rufus asked.

Operation of the telephones was much easier than it first appeared, once the callers got the hang of it. The only drawback to this particular telephone system was that Waynesville was the headquarters and all calls had to go through the switchboard there. If a man in Addie, for instance, needed a doctor from Sylva to care for a sick child, he had to call Waynesville and be plugged back to Sylva where he asked the operator to ring his call through. It was a rather ponderous system, Rufus thought, but it beat the daylights out of no system at all.

"These contraptions will never last," laughed one skeptic. "Why I can ride a hoss from Addie to Sylva and get a doctor to come to my house a whole lot quicker than I can get him by telephone."

Fortunately, that scoffer was wrong. It wasn't long before the wires were humming between Waynesville and Sylva and points in between and the telephones proved to be worth their weight in gold.

After Rufus learned to use the telephone, he called the sheriff's department in Waynesville and said that he would be arriving on the three-fifteen and would like the Haywood County sheriff to have Harley Woodson of Balsam meet him at the Waynesville station. "It's a matter of vital importance," Rufus said, "that I can't discuss on the telephone." All the telephone lines were party lines.

At the appointed time, Rufus stepped down from the platform of a passenger car and found Harley Woodson waiting, standing quietly beside his horse. With Rufus was Sheriff Clure, who had made it plain on the train coming over that he would stay out of it. This was to be Rufus's show, but Clure would guarantee the things that Rufus offered.

"Come with me," Rufus said, looking around at the depot area. "We need some privacy." Crossing the railroad tracks into the woods, away from prying eyes and ears, Rufus unrolled a blanket wrapped object and laid the rifle in question in Harley's arms.

"Harley," said Rufus, "I know this is Samson Reed's old rifle. I knew it the minute you clapped eyes on it the other day. You gave yourself away, turning pink and white, and then blue, and I knew I had hit your target.

"Now let me say this—and I ain't threatening you, Harley—the rifle has been identified by someone else, and I'm asking you again, 'Is this Samson Reed's old rifle'?"

"Are you tryin' to get me kilt, Rufus?"

"No, I ain't," Rufus answered. "I'm not gonna get you hurt in any way, neither you nor your family. You'll be given every protection in the world if you identify the gun, but you may face criminal charges if you don't. I ain't threatening you, Harley, I'm telling you the gospel. If you lie to me again about this gun, criminal abetting charges will be filed against you before I leave town.

"Howsomever, if you tell the truth and swear to it, you'll be protected, and so will your family."

"How will you protect us?"

"First of all, there's a hundred dollar reward that'll go to you as soon as you sign an affidavit that this was Samson's gun. A man can feed a lot of hungry children on a hundred dollars." Rufus showed him the hundred-dollar bill.

At the mention of a hundred dollar reward, Sheriff

Clure eyed Rufus sharply and then realized that Rufus had put up half of the reward money himself.

Rufus saw immediately that he had struck home. Harley's eyes widened and a slow smile spread over his mouth.

"After you swear by affidavit that this gun belonged to Samson Reed, I'll ask you another question and you'll be expected to answer it. I'll ask you who helped Samson put Sid's body in that rattlesnake den, and after that we'll take you and your family to the Buncombe County Home for Old Folks and hide you there till the trial's over. No one would think of looking for you there. After that, I don't see that you'll have anything to worry about.

"When it's all over you'll have the feeling that you've done a service for your home county and all the people in it.

"You can also bet that you'll never have to face Samson Reed again, because he'll be done away with. He'll get what he deserves. He'll either be put away for the rest of his natural life or he'll be taken to Raleigh and hung by the neck till he's dead."

By the gleam in Harley's eyes, Rufus could tell that the "extra bait" he had put into breaking the case had paid off.

"Harley, you'd be doing yourself, your family, and your friends a service that will be appreciated. We can't have people like Samson Reed running loose on our streets."

"Lemme make sure I got this straight," Harley said. "If I finger Samson and the other two, I'll get that hundred dollars for my family and Jackson County will throw in all the rest free of charge?"

"You won't have to be out a penny, Harley, and remember how good it'll feel to see your kids eating like all human beings ought to be able to eat. I don't see a single drawback for you in any of this.

"As soon as we get your signed affidavit, we'll arrest Samson Reed and the other two, put 'em behind bars, and throw the key away.

"You couldn't be given a better opportunity by the President of the United States. If fact, if he knowed about this, he'd be as proud of you as a speckled pup."

For the first time, Sheriff Clure spoke up. "Harley, Jackson County will stand behind every word that Rufus has said to you. Tomorrow morning, I will need you to come to my office in Sylva and sign the necessary papers. Tomorrow afternoon, we'll take you and your family to Asheville. The following morning, we will take Samson and his cohorts into custody and lock them away. And, by the way, Harley, you've told us everything but who helped Samson pull off the job. Who was it?"

"Bear Thomas and Jim Bull Jones," Harley said without batting an eye.

Lissa Silver©

THIRTY

That very morning, Rufus was feeling more like a peace officer, and in his mind the reason for this was his coming of age with his feeling and full admission of innocence he felt in his heart about the Hannessey boys.

"I just can't let it lie," he said. "I'm gonna have to go see them and straighten things out before I can do anything else."

The road up Kings Mountain to the Hannessey home was as beautiful as it was when he had made the earlier trip. Summer was now in full swing and more flowers were blooming, especially around the house. Mrs. Hannessey certainly had a green thumb.

He ground hitched Fred at the road and walked on up to the house. Deep within he felt that he had wronged the Hannesseys, especially Tom, and the sooner he straightened it out, the better off he would be in his own mind. If they wanted to be belligerent about his previous visit, he would have to take it and hold his tongue.

With that in mind, he approached the house and knocked on the front door.

In a moment, he heard someone coming, and when the door opened there stood Mrs. Hannessey.

"What do you want?" she snapped. "You wanna harass my boys some more."

"No, ma'am," he said. "Nothin' like that. I would like to talk to 'em if they're around."

"They're here," she said, stepping back. "Come on in."

Deep within, he felt he had wronged them by convicting them on a hunch of murder in his mind without a shred of cold, hard evidence.

He knew he had let his personal feelings interfere with his judgment, that his dislike of them, for whatever reason, had led to a conviction in his mind, and he planned to set that straight. He did not know how he would begin, however.

He had not long to ponder that question. Mrs. Hannessey backed away from the door and said, "Come on in the parlor."

"Mrs. Hannessey," Rufus said, "I'd like to have you come in, too, and listen to what I have to say. Then if you tell me to get lost, I will."

He felt better, knowing that she would sit and listen. He had expunged from his mind all his feelings of animosity toward them. How they felt about this he did not know, but deep within himself he was sure that he had grown through the experience, not just personally, but professionally also. He felt himself to be a better law enforcement officer, one who would never again jump to a rash conclusion without having evidence on the table before him.

The three boys came in together and took seats. Their mother was sitting halfway across the room, simply to hear, not to answer.

"Boys," Rufus began, "this is going to be hard for me to do, so be patient with me. I have an apology to make and

I'll just do it first. I am sorry that I have acted the way I have toward you, sorry for everything but punching Charlie and Pete in Velt's Café because they had said things about Sue and me that weren't true and if those things had come around to hurt Sue, then I might have taken further action." He told them that, and they both stared at the floor as if they were ashamed of what they had done.

"I'm sorry for convicting you in my mind before I had any evidence. I hope you'll lay it to my inexperience as a peace officer. You see, I wanted to convict you of the crime, but I didn't have the evidence.

"So I went off half-cocked. I will swear to you that the same will never happen to me again, and I hope you will accept my apology that I was totally wrong and away off base when I fingered you. If I said anything to you that I shouldn't have, I am sorry for that, too.

"I know now that you had nothing to do with Sid's death and am asking your forgiveness for the way I acted."

A thick hush fell over the room. It was Mrs. Hannessey who broke the silence.

"Well, say something, boys. If you've got anything on your minds, get it out. Say it so you all can get it straightened out, too."

"Well, I don't mind sayin'," Tom said, "that I knowed you was wrong all the way, but nothing I could of said at that time would have helped to make things right. Howsomever, I think you've done that this morning, and I, for one, accept your apology and say to you that if we can be of help in cracking this case, then we're on your side, Rufus."

The other two shook their heads in the affirmative, and Mrs. Hannessey appeared to be pleased.

"This took nerve for you to do, Rufus, but I think it shows character on your part," she said. "Ain't many men in authority who would take the blame on their own shoulders without trying to spread it around."

"It's all mine," Rufus said. "It's something I've got to work through myself, but I think I've prospered from the whole thing. I don't think you'll ever see me making this same mistake again."

"Put 'er there," Tom said, holding forward his hand, and Rufus shook it. The other two did the same.

"We're sorry for saying them things about you and Sue," Charlie said. "We know now that we was wrong. I think you and Sue have got something going, and I think it's good for both of you." Pete nodded in agreement.

Mrs. Hannessey stood. "Rufus, I'm right proud of you. Anybody else would have let this ride, but you've come out clean and I think you mean what you say."

"I agree," said Tom, "and if there's anything we can do to help you, just call on us. We'll be ready."

Leaving the house, a feeling of euphoria came over Rufus. He knew he had done the right thing, and perhaps had earned the respect of new friends by it.

He turned his full attention to Samson Reed as the main suspect in the death of Sid Hollifield. "We have the evidence to hang him, but it wouldn't hurt to get a little more," thought Rufus.

THIRTY-ONE

The "little more" Rufus was looking for came from an unexpected source. It was waiting in the presence of Preacher Snyder when Rufus returned to the office. The preacher was frowning; he had something on his mind that he appeared anxious to get off.

"It looks like something is heavy on your mind," said Rufus.

"Yes, it's heavy," the preacher said, "but I'm not sure I can divulge it to you because it would be classified in court as second-hand information."

"We'll take our chance on that," Rufus said. "Spit it out." He still had not recovered from the sermon the Reverend had preached about him.

"All right," Snyder seemed to make up his mind. "I was in Velt's yesterday for my afternoon coffee and couldn't help but overhear a conversation in the booth behind me."

"Go on."

"There were three men in the booth and one was Samson Reed," the preacher looked around furtively as if he feared someone else was listening in. "They talked low but I have good ears."

"Don't worry," Rufus said. "We're all alone."

"Here's what I overheard, but I am not sure who said what."

"Just give me the jist of the conversation."

"One of them said, 'Clure ain't too good in the woods. We can forget about him.'"

"Now I don't know who said the rest, but this is the way the conversation went: One said, 'We're gonna have to kill Rufus. He's the thorn in our side.'

"The other one said, 'I shore do like the looks of that gal.'

"'Why can't we do both?' the other one asked.

"'Both of what?" Mr. Reed asked him.

"'Take the girl,' the other said, "and that'll kill him. Get two birds with one stone.

"Any idea what girl they were talking about?" Rufus asked, feeling deep in his gut that he already knew the answer.

"It had to be Sue, I think, but that shouldn't be too hard for you to figure out."

"You say Reed was one, who were the other two?"

"I don't know. Never saw them before."

"Would you remember them on sight?"

"Hard to say because I had my back to them and was afraid to look around. That would have been a giveaway. And two of them had their backs to me. Never got a good look at their faces 'cept I got a glance when they left. I do remember this: one of the two had a scratchy voice."

"Mr. Snyder, that sounds like Jim Bull Jones," Rufus said. "You may have driven the last nails in their coffins."

"Don't talk to me like that."

"I know it ain't your lingo," Rufus said, "but it's mine—and the sheriff's. Did they give any idea when they wanted to try this?"

"I don't think so," the preacher said, "but they sounded anxious, like maybe they wanted to do it today or tomorrow."

Rufus stood and extended his hand to the rising preacher. "Sir, I thank you. Don't worry about what you told me being second-hand. I doubt it ever reaches the court room, but this may be the information we need to arrest them varmints. Don't tell what you heard to anyone else. That could get you hurt."

"You needn't worry about that," Rev. Snyder said, his voice shaking a bit. "I thought you ought to know, but I don't have the nerve to tell anyone else. Besides, you are authority. You ought to know things like this."

"Tell you what," Rufus said as an afterthought. "What you've told me may have more results than any sermon you could preach from your pulpit."

They shook hands and the preacher left first. Rufus poured another cup of coffee from the pot on the stove to help him digest what he had been told.

Sheriff Clure entered and Rufus told him of the conversation with the preacher.

"Then Reed's our man," said the sheriff.

Lissa Silver©

THIRTY-TWO

That was probably the week Rufus grew up, not only as a law enforcement officer, but as a man. He discovered his feelings for Sue were changing, either that or he began to realize what his feelings had been all along. He qualified that thought in his mind. It had begun only after Sid's death, when he recognized that with Sid gone, Sue's need for companionship would be greater than she had ever known. Rufus had enjoyed getting to know Sue that year and felt his feelings for her were growing.

Truly, he had no idea at first what love was beyond a family love. He loved his mother and had loved his brother, but he had never had a serious relationship with a woman. His lone intention had been to help Sue avoid the grip of loneliness.

Rufus now knew he felt something special for her but he was genuinely afraid to put the connotation of love to it because Sid had been gone for only a year. Was that time enough to admit he loved her? Did he really love her? What was love? He hadn't been hit over the head with an ax handle and told by the elf of love that he loved her. He had never even had a chance to know what love was before this.

He was working in the office, putting files in place, thanks to Sue's miraculous ability to teach him to read and write over one spring and summer, and he found that reading, especially, came clearer for him every day.

Suddenly Rufus dropped a file in the floor. Clure looked at him and saw consternation register on his face.

Rufus looked at his watch. It was nine-thirty in the morning. He said, "'...like maybe they wanted to do it today or tomorrow....'"

"What?" asked Clure.

"John," Rufus shouted, "the preacher said today or tomorrow. Quick, drive me to Sue's."

They hurried up the street in the Model T, pulled into Sue's yard, and saw her front door standing open. Rufus leapt from the car and ran up the steps. Inside the living room he found a jumble of overturned side tables, chairs, and furniture.

"Sue!" he shouted. "Sue!"

No answer came. Rufus ran back outside. "She's gone!" he shouted.

He ran to the next-door neighbor's house. Mrs. Sellers answered his knock. "Have you seen Sue?" Rufus asked. "Her living room's all tore up and she's gone."

"Yes, I'm glad you're here" Mrs. Sellers said. "She left with three men about a half hour ago. Looked like she didn't want to go. They had her hands tied, but there was nothing I could do."

Rufus leapt down the steps. "Get me back to the office," he said to Clure. "They've got her!"

In minutes Rufus climbed out of the car at the office. "Sheriff," he said, "I'm going after them, and I think I know where they're going. I could be wrong, so would you call the sheriff in Waynesville and have him start a search in Balsam for her? The other two men will be Bear Thomas and Jim Bull Jones. I'll need you to drive over there, too, and as soon as Sheriff Jackson gets the search going, bring him over to Maggie Valley in your car. Bring him to Presley's Store. I'll try to be there by then, and I've an idea I'll need him. Tell him I'll have a horse for him."

Maggie Valley was in Haywood County, in Sheriff Jackson's jurisdiction.

Rufus saw Jim Ryan coming up the street. "Jim!" he shouted. "Come over here." He told Ryan what had happened and added, "Go round up two or three more good men and bring them to the stable. That'll be enough for a posse."

Ryan headed up the street and Rufus ran to the livery. "Saddle up a half-dozen of your best horses," he said to the liveryman. "I need 'em for a posse. And throw a saddle on Fred. I'll need it where I'm going. Need to carry a rifle with me."

The man went to work and Rufus ran back to the office. He took a Winchester from the rack, grabbed a box of ammunition, and ran back to the livery.

Jim Ryan came a few minutes later with James Lee Blanton, Clyde Rector, and Bobby Jones. "All I could find," he said.

"They'll be enough. Pick out one of them saddled horses," he said to all, "and let's hit the trail. We've some riding to do. One of you bring an extra horse. The Haywood sheriff's gonna meet us in Maggie Valley."

Up the Fisher Creek road they went at a brisk trot. "Don't run the horses," Rufus said. "We've got a long way to go, and part of it's gonna be up and down a mountain or two."

At the end of the Fisher Creek road above Rufus's house, they turned onto the path that zig-zagged up the mountain to Waterrock Knob, and from there they would take the Campbell Creek trail into Maggie.

"Let's don't punish the horses," Rufus said. "Follow me." He started up the trail at a trot, and by walking the horses through the steepest parts and trotting them the rest of the way, they reached the Knob in an hour and a half and headed down Campbell Creek toward Maggie.

When they reached Presley's Store, Alaska Presley, who had operated it since the death of her husband, Hubert, was standing outside, talking with Sheriff Clure and Haywood County Sheriff Tom Jackson.

"Hello, Rufus," Alaska said as the party rode up. "How's your ma?"

"She's doing all right," he said, "but you look mighty peaked."

Rufus turned toward the men and said, "We'll rest the horses for thirty minutes, men. Grain 'em a little, water 'em, and we'll hit the trail again."

"Have you seen Samson Reed and his two pals?" Rufus asked Alaska.

"Yes, they were here and nearly scared me to death, but when they heard Sheriff Clure's car coming, they hustled across the road and into the woods."

"Was Sue with them?"

"Yes, she was."

"Did she look all right?"

"Yes. I don't think they've harmed her yet."

"Where are we going?" asked Sheriff Jackson, "to Cherokee?"

"Nope," Rufus answered. "Samson'll go down Jonathan Creek and head into the Smokies from there."

"What makes you think that? He could go into the Smokies from Cherokee."

"I think he's gone down Jonathan Creek because that's the way I'd go if I was runnin' from the law," Rufus said.

"We'll head up by that old Ghost Town where Harmon Teaster killed that bunch of outlaws, cut over to Cataloochee Divide and look for his tracks there. That's his quickest way to get into the deep Smokies and if we let him get in there, we'll never find him."

"Well, you run things the way you see fit," said Sheriff Jackson. "You lead and we'll follow. Reckon I'm along just to make things legal."

"That's right, Sheriff, and we appreciate you being here," Rufus said. "We may have some killing to do and I don't want to get charged with murder."

Rufus turned to Alaska. "Would you get me a dope, Alaska? I'm right thirsty," he said, and she returned to the store and brought several cold, bottled drinks for all the men.

Rufus fished in his pocket for money and Alaska said, "No charge, Rufus. Do you need any food from the store? I can bag up some."

"No, thanks," Rufus said. "I'm hopin' we won't be in the woods that long."

After a half-hour, the horses were rested and frisky, anxious to get back on the trail. Clure returned to Sylva.

The posse cut up the dirt road to Ghost Town, crossed behind it onto Fie Top Road and on to Cataloochee Divide.

There they stopped again to rest the horses, and Rufus stayed aboard Fred. "You wait here," he said to the men. "I'll go down and look for tracks, see if they've crossed over yet. I ain't gonna let 'em get her in the deep woods where they can have their way with her and we'd have to track 'em to find 'em. If I can pick up their trail here, we'll catch up with them. They won't expect us to be this close behind. Fact is, they might think they've lost us already. I'm hoping that's what they're thinking. That might slow 'em down."

Riding the spine of the Divide, Rufus found their trail within minutes. He dismounted and examined the hoof prints. "Yep," he said to himself, "ain't fifteen minutes old. We can catch 'em in a mile or two."

He leapt aboard Fred, rode back within sight of the others and beckoned them to follow him. Soon they were on the tracks and making good time. Once, a half-hour later, Rufus called a halt, examined the tracks again, and announced, "They're no more than minutes ahead. We'll catch 'em in the woods."

Rather than ride straight across the clearing, as Reed had led the others, they rode around the edge of the clearing, passing behind all the trees they could. Reed would not expect them to come that way. He would look for them to come straight across the clearing.

When they reached the tracks where the fugitives had gone into the forest, Rufus hauled up short and dismounted. The others joined him.

"I'm going in after them," Rufus said softly. "They'll have to stop and water their horses at that first creek. It ain't more than a hundred yards from here. You men stay here and if you hear shooting, come a'running."

Rufus entered the forest silently, watching that he stepped on no sticks that would announce his arrival to the outlaws.

He was right. They were dismounted at the creek. Bear Thomas and Jim Bull Jones had already watered their mounts and had grabbed Sue, who screamed. Off to the side, watching and laughing at them, Reed let his horse drink its fill from the stream.

Rufus walked into the glade and Reed saw him immediately. He stepped away from his horse with a hand on his holstered pistol.

"You'll get yours first," he said to Rufus, "and the girl will get hers next."

He drew the pistol, but before it cleared the holster, Rufus's forty-five was out in a flash and his bullet hammered Reed in the stomach. The report of the pistol shot brought the posse running.

Reed backed up a step and, trying to raise his pistol into firing position, he took another hammer blow to the chest. The posse saw Reed drop his weapon in the creek and fall backward into the water.

He was dead.

At the first shot, Bear Thomas and Jim Bull Jones crashed into the forest and disappeared, running at top speed to get away.

"Let's get 'em," Bobby Jones yelled.

"No!" Sheriff Jackson shouted. "Let 'em go. The forest will take care of them."

The posse dragged Reed out of the creek, noticing that Rufus's first shot had hit him squarely in the stomach and the second had pierced his heart.

At that moment Sue ran into Rufus's arms. Rufus squeezed her with the biggest bear hug the posse had ever seen. Then Sue turned her faced upward and kissed Rufus full in the mouth. He responded, and for a few moments they clutched each other with tears rolling out of their eyes. Then Sue sank her head into his chest and continued to sob.

"It's all right now, Sue," Rufus said. "Did they harm you?"

"No, I'm all right," she answered, wiping tears off her cheeks. "They didn't have time. We stopped at Alaska Presley's store, but when they heard Sheriff Clure's car coming, they threw me back in the saddle, mounted quickly, and rode across the road into the woods and got away."

Rufus looked into Sue's eyes. "Sue," he said, "I love you. I know it now. I knew it all the time, but didn't know what it was."

She melted into his arms again. "And I love you, Rufus, with all my heart and soul."

"What are we going to do about Thomas and Jones?" Clyde Rector interrupted. "They'll get away."

"They won't get far," said Sheriff Jackson. "Neither of them is Dan'l Boone. They don't know the forest. They'll either get killed by a bear or find a way out and show up back in civilization.

"I'll put reward notices out for them as soon as I get back to Waynesville."

Jim Ryan and James Lee Blanton caught up Samson Reed's horse and tied his body across its back. "We'll let the sheriff take him back to Waynesville," James Lee said. "This is his county. He'll do away with him or have him buried somewhere."

"That Rufus is something else," James Lee said. "I never saw such shooting."

"He had something to shoot for," Jim Ryan said.

"What do you mean?" James Lee asked.

"Sue," Ryan responded, watching Rufus and Sue lock together again in a long, long kiss.

Lissa Silver©

THIRTY-THREE

Rufus quit his job as deputy sheriff, and six months passed quickly, during which Rufus and Sue eloped to Asheville and were married; the Barker brothers finished fencing, clearing, and resowing Rufus's farm, and refurbished and painted the old farm house.

Rufus's whiskey still became a thing of the past, smashed to bits by Rufus, himself, with an ax. Seventeen mares and three great studs grazed in the pasture, the new barn sheltered them adequately, and colts were due in the spring.

Bear Thomas had been mauled to death by a bear in the Smokies, and while the bear was having his way, Jim Bull Jones escaped, made his way out of the woods, and at the moment was spending the rest of his natural life in a cell in Central Prison in Raleigh.

Rufus could read, write, and cipher as well as a school teacher, and perhaps the greatest accomplishment, at least the one that Sue, Rufus, and Paralee looked forward to the most, was that Sue was heavy with child.

Sheriff Clure maintained the peace. There was little else to do after the excitement died down. Jackson County settled back into its daily routines.

Clure announced he would retire at the end of his present term as sheriff and the county expected Rufus to run for the office that November. All he would say, however, was "When the baby comes, I'll have enough to do, runnin' my family and the R.S.P. Ranch."

Rufus was elected chairman of their Sunday school when Clyde Preston gave up the job, and Sue was proud as a speckled pup because Rufus relished the job.

Clure hired Hovie Cutter, Rufus's woodcutting helper, as his new deputy.

Things went well for a couple of weeks until one morning the widow May Sprinkle hurried into the sheriff's office.

"Sheriff!" she almost shouted. "I need help!"

"What's wrong, May?" Clure asked, leaping from his seat. "What's happened?"

"My little Bobby is up on the roof and won't get down," she gushed. "Every time I call him, he runs to the other side of the roof."

"Bobby? Who's Bobby?" Clure asked.

"He's my half-growed tom cat."

Clure settled back in his seat, smiling, looked at Hovie Cutter, and calmly said to him: "Get Rufus!"

LaVergne, TN USA
18 September 2009
158359LV00003B/12/P

9 781566 642736